THE BILLIONAIRE'S BRIBE

JAMBREA JO JONES

The Billionaire's Bribe
ISBN # 978-1-83943-857-8
©Copyright Jambrea Jo Jones 2020
Cover Art by Erin Dameron-Hill ©Copyright March 2020
Interior text design by Claire Siemaszkiewicz
Pride Publishing

This is a work of fiction. All characters, places and events are from the author's imagination and should not be confused with fact. Any resemblance to persons, living or dead, events or places is purely coincidental.

All rights reserved. No part of this publication may be reproduced in any material form, whether by printing, photocopying, scanning or otherwise without the written permission of the publisher, Pride Publishing.

Applications should be addressed in the first instance, in writing, to Pride Publishing. Unauthorised or restricted acts in relation to this publication may result in civil proceedings and/or criminal prosecution.

The author and illustrator have asserted their respective rights under the Copyright Designs and Patents Acts 1988 (as amended) to be identified as the author of this book and illustrator of the artwork.

Published in 2020 by Pride Publishing, United Kingdom.

No part of this book may be reproduced, scanned, or distributed in any printed or electronic form without permission. Please do not participate in or encourage piracy of copyrighted materials in violation of the authors' rights. Purchase only authorised copies.

Pride Publishing is an imprint of Totally Entwined Group Limited.

If you purchased this book without a cover you should be aware that this book is stolen property. It was reported as "unsold and destroyed" to the publisher and neither the author nor the publisher has received any payment for this "stripped book".

THE
BILLIONAIRE'S
BRIBE

Dedication

Thank you, Susan,
for pushing me to write this story.
Mercy, thank you for the help you've given me.
This one is for you two.

Chapter One

Remington Marlow glared down at the phone on his desk as if it might jump up and bite him. His father was on speaker, spouting nonsense too early in the morning. He needed more coffee for this conversation.

"Damn it, Dad. This is ridiculous." Slamming his hand on the desk, Remington Marlow picked up the handset.

The whole company didn't need to know his business. Jackson Marlow might be his father, but he was out of his ever-loving mind to think Remi was going to just get in line with this cockamamie plan of him settling down. He was very happy his father was at the main office about five minutes away and not down the hall, because he would have done something rash, like throttle him. He hated arguing about his dating habits...again. It wasn't like he was a kid anymore. He'd just had his thirty-sixth birthday.

"No, it isn't," Jackson declared. "I gave up the hope of an heir when I found out you were gay, but there are options out there, Remi."

"Dad—"

"Don't you 'Dad' me. I watch the news and see the kids that need adopting—or you could even go with a surrogate. I'm not saying you need to have kids now, but I won't have you fucking your way through all the men in Fort Wayne."

"I have not fucked my way through *all* the men." Remi rubbed his temple.

His dad sighed and continued his tirade. "I want you to settle down. Date a man. Get to know him. Fall in love and get married. I want you to have what I did. The years I had with your mother were the best times of my life and I would give anything to have them back."

"I know, Dad. I know. I miss her too," Remi agreed.

"Maybe I did wrong by you, giving you everything you ever wanted, making sure you got a generous monthly stipend until your billions release to you. Well, it stops now. You're going to have to learn to live on your paycheck alone without any other money from me. I'm cutting you off if you don't do something about your life. That's final. You start actively dating someone and I will let your trust release in full on your fortieth birthday and I won't stop your monthly allowance."

"Is this why you put the clause into my trust? I understand payouts, but who makes a person wait until they're forty for the final one?" Remi wanted to throw the phone across the room. He was so frustrated with the conversation. He was almost forty and his dad was still giving him an allowance.

"You're lucky I didn't add in a marriage stipulation from the beginning, Remi." His dad threw more heat on to the fire happening right now in Remi's body.

"I knew you were controlling, but this takes the cake." Remi pinched the bridge of his nose. "You know Mom wanted me to have that money when I turned twenty-one. All of it. No allowance. Full control."

"Yes, but I fought her on it. I wanted you to be more mature, and twenty-one is still too young to have that kind of money. When she died, I knew I'd done the right thing. You were even more self-destructive."

"I'd just lost my mother, but that's beside the point. You do know I'm a grown man, right? Running a multibillion-dollar company?" Remi dropped his face into his hand.

His head pounded. He'd drunk too much at the club the previous night and taken some twink home. Remi couldn't remember his name, but he had a nice tight ass on him. *That* was worth remembering. His dad voice jolted him out of his hangover memory fuzz.

"I do. I also know you blow money like there's no tomorrow."

"You're making it seem like we're going to run out any day now."

His head hurt, he wasn't even awake yet and now he was thinking about his mom… *Coffee.* God, a cup of coffee would be so good right now, but he hadn't had a chance to grab a cup yet and he couldn't get his secretary Sara Jo to get it when he was on the phone. *Fuck my life.*

"You never know what the future holds, son."

"You're lucky I love you, old man." Remi might be exasperated with his father, but he did love him. He would have to work at talking him out of this stupid idea that he needed to fall in love. Usually it only took a couple weeks to bring him around.

Remi was quite happy with his life. He didn't want to settle down. He didn't want to be someone's sugar daddy. How would he know if a guy wanted him for more than his money? He'd made that mistake before. It had broken his heart when he'd found out that his bank balance was all that his ex had wanted him for.

When the flavor of the week heard his name, they were predictably all over him for a relationship. Fort Wayne wasn't that big and, even in Indianapolis, the Marlow name was known in certain circles. He wasn't a relationship type of guy—not anymore, not after Harry.

"You're lucky that I love you back. I wouldn't be throwing down an ultimatum if I wasn't concerned. And don't think you're going to talk me out of it. As the executor of the living trust your mother and I set up for you, I've already had the lawyers draw up paperwork stating the new terms. There was a clause in the trust."

"Yes, I know. How you talked Mom into letting you set up payout terms as well as allowing you to change it as you saw fit, I'll never know. I'm not happy, Dad." Remi couldn't express that enough.

"I didn't think you would be. But I love you and want you to be happy."

Damn it. Remi didn't want to date. He loved his dad and knew he was coming from a good, if misguided, place. They were getting ready to expand the company. He had enough on his plate with that. He took his work seriously. Sure, he liked to have fun and that took money—more money than he could make pulling a paycheck from the company. The small gift he'd gotten from his grandfather when he'd died wouldn't last forever, and he'd already gotten his allowance for the month. His money in the trust wouldn't release to him in full until he was forty. He only had a few more years, which was probably why his dad was pulling this crap now.

"What if I decide to say 'fuck it all' and live off my paycheck?" Remi sat back in his chair with a slight grin on his face. He *could* do it. Would it be easy? No, but he was smart enough to figure it out.

"I've seen your bills." Jackson snorted. "I'll give you a week to make your decision. Just remember… You don't get your trust money for four more years, unless I deem you unfit to get it at that time and make you wait even longer."

He'd had his heart ripped out before and he wasn't going to let it happen again. As much as he might want what his father'd had, it wasn't in the cards for him. His father had met his mom when they had still been in high school. Money had never come between them, not like it had with him and Harry. Remi's heart just couldn't take that kind of abuse. He was fine by himself and he needed to convince his father to leave his personal life alone.

"I *am* happy, Dad."

"No, son, you're well fucked. That doesn't always equal happy." Jackson sighed into the phone. "Money can help, but it won't keep you warm at night or coddle you when you're sick."

"A bit crude dad, but sex does make me happy." Well, as happy as he could be.

"No, it means you are satisfied for the moment. I want you fulfilled for a lifetime." His dad's voice was almost a whisper.

"And if I can't find that?" Remi whispered back.

"I want you to at least try. Is that really too much to ask?"

"Yes, it is. You might think you know my life, but you don't. And I don't have time for this. I'm in the middle of negotiations to take over the steel company. You know having a place to pull our metal from could cut cost in the fabrication end of the company. It's a big deal and searching for a guy to date isn't going to be that easy." Remi blew out a breath. He was getting upset again.

"The steel company isn't going anywhere. The deal is almost done. If you can take the time to go find a fuck-buddy, you can find the time to date. I want to see you at least try. I don't want you to end up like me, an old man who lost his love and will die alone. You're almost forty and I'm not getting any younger. If you have kids, I'd like to still be able to be a good grandpa."

"Fuck." Remi rubbed his chest. His dad wasn't pulling any punches.

"Yeah, I got deep on you. After your mom passed, I was a wreck. She was my soul mate. I'm lonely. I don't want you to hit sixty and still be looking for one-night stands. I want you to have someone to come home to, who will love you as much as your mother loved me."

"Emotional blackmail." Remi laughed. If he didn't, he might cry. Thinking about his mom made him emotional. Thinking about her with little sleep and no coffee? It was going to kill him.

"I'll do what I have to."

His father had to be grinning on the other end of the line. Remi could hear it in his voice.

"Dad…" Remi sighed in frustration.

"Remi…"

"Fine. Whatever." He understood where his dad was coming from and it sucked. Remi hated that his father was alone. He tried to see him as much as he could, because it really was only the two of them against the world, but he knew he was no replacement for his mother.

"All right. We still on for dinner later tonight?" His dad sounded hopeful.

"Yes, I'll bring the wine." Remi wasn't going to stop seeing his dad, no matter what.

Jackson cleared his throat. "Love you, son."

"Love you too, Dad." He hung up the phone and sat back in his chair. The headache he'd been fighting all morning was growing stronger. He closed his eyes, rubbing his temple.

What the hell am I going to do?

He didn't want to have his heart broken again, but he also wanted to give his father what he wanted. *Shit.* He was going to have to date and show his dad that he was serious. He could live without the money. This ultimatum was about more than money. But where the fuck was he going to find someone suitable to date? He was happy being a playboy. Sure, he really didn't get out as much as he had in the past. He was settling down in his life, just not in the way his dad wanted him to.

Remi would have to think about it later. The first thing he needed was coffee before he went over his notes. He pushed his chair back and waved at Sara Jo as he passed.

Remi loved running the fabrication shop. It was all his. He'd built it up to where it was. They had been losing potential profit because they needed to pay other shops around town to do their steel work. And now he was going to expand his division even more, so they wouldn't have to spend so much on the metal they were working with. Usually his dad would take care of adding on to the company, but the fab shop was his baby and he'd had the idea to add on when one of the steel suppliers was having a cash flow issue. His company took in small walk-in projects, big company projects, work for the construction end of the company and unique things. They were now the go-to shop in town.

The coffee was in the breakroom located in the middle of the building so the detailers — the ones who drew up the blueprints and made sure a steel structure would stand on its own — could get to it just as easily as he could. He at least knew everyone's names, even if he didn't see or talk to each of them every day. He trusted his staff to get the job done.

Sara Jo was in the middle of planning a cookout for the company, one of her duties as his admin. It was something Remi liked to do to show appreciation for all the hard work everyone did. It had been a rough couple months with hot jobs and overtime. The shop was crazy when the local General Motors plant shut down so they could get in and do some repairs and put in additional ducts. There was always so much to do for shut down work. The railroad needed steel or a local school needed handrail before they opened the doors for students. Being a metal-job shop meant they got all kinds of projects. Someone had walked in just the other day and wanted a custom fire pit. Those kind of jobs were fun, but they had to work them in on days when they also were juggling big jobs such as building a tower for the high school, so the band instructor could see the full field or the football coach would watch the players, or getting steel over to the college that the construction division needed to fix the roof.

They all needed a break. If they didn't get it, safety could become an issue. If Sara Jo hadn't been in the middle of working on the cookout, he might have asked her to get his coffee, but he tried not to ask her for menial favors too often. His legs weren't broken and he could serve himself. He only sometimes asked in a coffee emergency, like now.

Remi retrieved some of the much-needed brew, headed back to his desk and shut the door. He had a couple of deadlines he was working on and wanted to get the drawings together for the people he had a meeting with for one of his pet projects, to update the abandoned upstairs of the historic Embassy Theater building. Closing himself in with work would keep his mind off his personal problems.

After what seemed like only a few minutes but was probably longer, there was the knock on his door that pulled him out of his concentration.

"Come in," Remi called.

Sara Jo ducked around the door. "Hey, bossman, do you have a minute to talk to Elros Carter?"

Remi tossed down his pencil. "Yeah, sure, I have a few minutes." He rubbed his eyes. The headache from the morning was gone, but his eyes were tired from pouring over the theater-project drawings. He knew the name, Elros Carter, but couldn't put a face to it.

"Want me to refill your cup?" Sara Jo smiled at him.

He looked at his coffee mug and thought about it for a second, "No, I'm good. I think I've had enough for today."

"All right. Remember… Your meeting is at one-thirty." She gave him a small smile.

"I thought it was at one?" Remi looked over his calendar.

"It was, but it was moved back because Mr. Johnson had a conflict." She tsked at him, like he should have remembered.

"All right, I guess I have more than a few minutes for Mr. Carter. Send him in." Remi waved her off.

Sara Jo nodded then opened the door, admitting a tall black-haired guy with the darkest brown eyes Remi had ever seen. *Man, he's tall*. He had to be at least six foot three and had a lean body. The type of guy he'd usually go for.

Hot damn.

Now he put the face with the name. He must really be tired. He knew who Elros was. Remi employed ten detailers, and he knew all their names. When Elros had been hired, Remi had made sure to work with one of the other detailers to keep himself out of trouble.

He didn't date people who worked for him. There was a reason for that. It was called a lawsuit, and he wanted nothing to do with one of those. But a plan started to form. He knew it was a bad idea, but it could get his father off his back. And, really, he wouldn't be breaking his dating rule, not if it the whole thing was made up.

A fake boyfriend? That, he could do.

Chapter Two

El stood in front of Mr. Marlow's desk until he was asked to have a seat. He fiddled with the cuffs of his shirt and smoothed his pants legs in order to calm himself. It wasn't working. His heart pounded and he could feel the sweat dripping down his back. El had a crush on the big boss, not that it would ever go anywhere. He was a minion in the company, while Remington Marlow was a billionaire who could have any man he wanted. Plus, he was here for work, not a date. He needed to start talking and ask for the overtime. That was what he was there for and he still needed to go home to check on his mom. He didn't have time to think about something that would never happen. He lived in the here and now. Fantasy hadn't been part of his life for a very long time.

Then Remington Marlow did the most horrible thing. He smiled.

God.

Did El's heart stop beating in his chest? Because he couldn't catch his breath. His brain stopped working and, for a brief second, he couldn't even remember why he was there. *Shit.* He should leave before he embarrassed himself. He'd be out of job faster than he could blink if he started coming on to the boss.

"So, Mr. Carter, what can I help you with?" Remington steepled his fingers together, his focus laser sharp.

"I—" El cleared his throat. "You see, I was wondering if I could get in some more overtime. We have a few projects I could be working on after hours."

There. He'd gotten it out of his mouth without too much effort. Hopefully, his face wasn't red and he wasn't making a fool out of himself. That would totally suck—and not in the good way. He was a professional, damn it, and he was going to act like one.

"I see. Let me check a couple of figures." Mr. Marlow turned to his computer, clicked several keys and frowned. "I'm sorry. It looks like you have reached your allotted overtime allowance." He clicked the mouse a few times and frowned again.

El covered his face with his hands and closed his eyes. He was going to need to get a second job and he couldn't afford to leave his mom alone anymore, even if she was okay with it. He needed to be there to help her. They didn't need anyone else, because if he called hospice, it would be like he'd given up. One of the perks of his job was the opportunity to work from home. The company had laptops they used to log into the system so he could work on details for the steel fabrication he was doing. He tried not to abuse that privilege, but with his mom being so sick, he did what he had to so he could be there for her. A lot of the overtime could be accomplished at home, and that was what he'd been hoping for, not the need to go out and try to find side work.

Can this day get any worse?

He sighed, wiped his hands on his thighs, stood up and held out his hand. "I'm sorry for bothering you. Thank you for your time, Mr. Marlow."

"Don't rush off." Mr. Marlow put his hands together with his pointer fingers tapping his lips. "Sit back down, please."

His boss stared intently at him. It made him a tad uncomfortable. El turned to leave. He had to get out. *Now.* If he didn't, he might do something he'd regret. Then he'd be looking for another job altogether.

"I really need to get to my lunch. I have —"

Mr. Marlow stood and walked toward him. "What if I had a proposition for you? I don't want to pry, but how bad do you need the hours?" He moved to the edge of his desk and sat down, his arms folded across his chest.

That surprised him. Just what was his boss going to ask?

"It's personal." El went back to the chair and sat down. Something in the way Mr. Marlow looked at him made him uncomfortable. El couldn't place it and he couldn't afford to offend the boss. If he had to start fresh at a new company, he'd be deeper in debt than he was now. He was trying to do his best with what he had, and he hadn't asked for any family or medical leave. No one at the company, except for Sara Jo, knew about his mom, and he planned on keeping it that way.

Mr. Marlow held up both hands. "I have an idea I want to run by you. I want to first state that what I'm about to ask will in no way affect your job if you say no. Do you understand?"

El nodded. He had a funny feeling in his gut, like something was crawling inside that shouldn't be there.

What in the world is he going to ask me?

"Okay. Good. I want you to move in with me."

"What?" El stood up so fast that the chair he was in scooted back.

"Well, that came out a bit wrong. I want you to *pretend* to be my boyfriend. Move in with me for a period of time and help me to convince my father that I'm settled in and dating." Mr. Marlow stared into his eyes.

"I— What—? No— How?" He was in a nightmare. The next thing he knew, he'd be naked in school trying to answer an unanswerable question.

"You don't have to answer right now. Take a day or so. Wait! You don't have a boyfriend, do you?"

Now he asks?

El sat back down. A boyfriend? Like he had time for that. And that shouldn't be the first thing he thought of. He should be outraged at the proposition.

"Look. Go to lunch. Think about it. When you have an answer, let me know. We can go into more details at that time. I'll let you know what to expect. We can draw up a contract. Like I said, this will not affect your job. You'd be doing me a favor and I can help you with the extra money you need. We really don't have the extra overtime in the budget right now, so don't think I'm using this as an excuse."

This time, Mr. Marlow stood and held out a hand. El stood, shook it, turned and left.

He really had nothing else to say. He couldn't. His mind was blown. He'd gone in looking for more work and he'd come out with a vague notion of being boyfriends with the boss. He had to keep thinking.

Pretend. This wasn't going to be something real. And he had his mother to think about. What was she going to say about all this? There was no way he'd lie to her about anything. She had so little time left.

* * * *

A short while later El walked into the house. He didn't make a lot of noise because he wasn't sure if his mom was awake or not. It'd take him a few minutes to get her broth ready anyway. She might not want to eat, but he had to try.

He walked to the kitchen and took out the pot he'd cooked that weekend. He always made a lot, so her food prep was easier during the week. He'd still need something for his own meal, but he could grab that on the way out of the door. He'd eat on the way back to the office. It was a habit he'd gotten into when his mom had gotten worse.

El took a bowl down from the cupboard. He wished he could let it warm up over the stove, but he didn't have time. If he had the money... *Money*. Yeah, maybe he shouldn't go there, because he'd be tempted to run back to the office and agree to whatever his boss wanted. There was no way he should rush into a situation like that. What would happen with his mom? He had to talk to her first. It was a crazy idea anyway. El wondered how Mr. Marlow had come up with it. Maybe he should ask that question before he gave an answer. He filled the bowl and turned to the microwave to heat it. She didn't like it too hot, but if she was asleep and he left it on her table, it would be better for it to start out scalding. He wanted her to be awake because he had to talk to her, get her to talk him out of it.

But what if it was a good deal? What if he could get the money for the experimental drug? Maybe even get a nurse in a few days a week... El could use all the help he could get.

If it seemed too good to be true, it usually was. He'd heard that from his mom over the years. The beeping of the microwave made him jump.

"El, is that you?" He barely heard her voice coming from her room.

"Yes, Mom. I've got some soup for you."

"I'm not hungry."

She sounded better than she had this morning. Her voice wasn't breaking up and her breathing sounded better. Maybe it would be a good day. He took a potholder out of the drawer and lifted the soup from the microwave.

"Maybe you'll get hungry. It's too hot right now anyway." El walked into her room.

His mom sat up in the bed. She was weak and really needed to eat. If she didn't, she wouldn't keep her strength up and could become too ill for the trial drug.

"Okay. You can set it over there." His mom pointed at her nightstand.

El would do anything for his mom, even move in with his boss so he could have the money to make her better. Was he really thinking about it? Yes, he was. To extend his mother's life, he'd do just about anything. He wasn't ready to lose her to cancer. *Fuck cancer.*

"What has you thinking so hard over there?"

El shook his head and moved to the recliner by the bed so he could sit down.

"I asked for more overtime." He shrugged like it was no big deal.

"Oh, El, no. You need more time to have fun."

"What I need is for you to get better." He smiled at her.

"You only live once. I should know better than most. There is a lot of stuff I wished I would have done before I got this bad." She plucked at her blanket, worrying it between her fingers.

"Like what?" El was curious. His mom had never brought up the things she'd wished she'd done, probably because she hadn't been able to do them as a single mother and she knew he'd blame himself for that.

"Traveled. I would not have cared if I didn't have the money. I would go anyway—Paris, New Zealand, Japan. So many places… You know, once I'm gone—"

"Don't talk like that." He couldn't handle thinking about life without her.

"You have to be realistic, son. Once I'm gone, you should travel—or do something you've wanted to do but thought you couldn't. Enjoy life."

El hated it when she talked like that. His stomach hurt, and he wanted to cry. She was his mom. She couldn't leave him. Not yet.

"Okay." It was easier to just agree with her for now, so they could get off the morbid topic. "Something interesting did happen at work. When I asked for the overtime, my boss told me I'd already had my allotted quota."

"Good!"

El barked out a surprise laugh. That was his mom.

"Anyway, he told me he had a proposition for me."

"This is getting interesting." His mom rubbed her hands together.

"Just wait. He wants me to move in with him."

"Wait! Are you dating? You didn't tell me you had a boyfriend." She looked both confused and a little displeased.

"No, we're not dating. He wants me to be his 'pretend' boyfriend."

"Why?"

"I didn't ask him. I was too shocked at the offer. He told me that he'd pay me, since I need the money. I'd just have to move in and pretend we're together."

"Do it."

El was shocked. "What? You've got to be kidding me. Mom!"

"I am not kidding you. Do it."

"What about you?"

"Call hospice."

"No." He couldn't do that. It wasn't time.

"Then call one of those nurses. I'm pretty sure it's in the insurance. Look into it. But I want to do this. Do it for me. I don't want you to be alone."

"Mom, didn't you hear the 'pretend' part?"

"I did. But things can happen. You never know. Trust your mother."

"This isn't a romance novel. I'd move in for a predetermined amount of time. We'd sign a contract. Everything would be above board"

"It better not be. I've seen your boss. He's hot."

"You *must* be feeling better." El sighed.

"Life is short. Have fun."

Have fun. Do I even know how to do that anymore? If he moved in with his boss for anyone, it'd be his mom. But at what cost?

Chapter Three

That could have gone better.

Remi thumped his head on the desk a couple of times. It didn't help. He should have thought it through better. He should go to lunch and forget about the whole thing, chalk it up to a low blood sugar hallucination, not that he'd ever had one before. But today was as good a time as any for his first. He wanted to make his dad happy, but the fake boyfriend wasn't going to last anyway. It was a stupid idea to think he could fake a relationship for any period of time. Remi needed to cut expenses and just live off his paycheck until his trust money really was his, show his dad he could do it. Maybe that would get his father's attention enough for him to realize that Remi didn't need someone in his life—not now, maybe never. He was gay. Why did he have to live up to some heteronormative idea of what a relationship should be?

My dad. Remi sighed. He knew his father had his best interests at heart, but sometimes he made things *so* difficult.

He did remember the look on Elros' face. It had gone from shock to thinking about it. *Would it really be so bad?*

The confusion was too much. He was going to leave the office and clear his head. Spur-of-the-moment stuff always got him in trouble, like the time he'd convinced his cousin to go cliff diving. He'd thought it'd be fun and he'd jumped—not thought, just did it. His cousin had passed out, hit his head on a rock and had to be carried off to the hospital. If he'd known how afraid of heights Michael had been, he might not have done it. *Maybe.* But it was that devil-may-care attitude that seemed to haunt him at times.

A knock on his door was a welcome distraction.

"Are you ready for your appointment?" Sara Jo peered around the door.

"Is it one-thirty already?" *Well, there went lunch.*

"Just about. I wanted to make sure you had time to look over your notes before they got here."

"I'm good. If you'd get the conference room ready, I'll go ahead and bring my prints in."

"All done. The coffee is brewed and I have some water ready to go in the fridge if someone wants anything. I'll double-check when they get here."

"Okay, thanks. I'll head in."

"How did the meeting go with El?"

Remi had forgotten that the two were friends. He should have remembered that. *Damn.* This could make things worse, because there was no way it would work if Sara Jo could see through the lie. No one could know. If they did, his dad would find out. He always did. It was, like...his superpower.

"Fine. Just fine."

"Okay, good." Sara Jo shut the door behind her.

He would have to talk to El and make sure he didn't say anything, even if he didn't agree to it. Because, if he didn't, Remi was going to have to go hunting for someone else. He didn't have the time to worry about something like that. El would be perfect. He knew the hours needed for the job. He was easy to talk to. But there was Sara Jo. They were good friends. Would she even believe they were dating? How much did El really tell her?

Maybe they would be more compatible than either of them knew. But, for now, he needed all his focus to be on business. He couldn't go into the meeting with his head going in another direction. There would be time for that later, though he didn't have a follow-up with Elros planned. He could call El to his office. *No.* No, he couldn't. He'd told El he'd give him a day or so. If he pushed it, it would look bad.

El was a good detailer. He worked hard and produced great drawings. Plus, he could check other people's work and find mistakes like no one else on his team. Remi might not talk to all the detailers every day, but he knew who could do what. Marlow as a company couldn't afford to lose someone so experienced.

Remi wished he'd asked what El had needed the money for. It could have helped him decide what to offer. At this point, he'd give El whatever he needed, *if* he agreed.

And again—no more of this. He had work to do. Remi picked the rolled-up drawings from his desk and headed for the conference room. This meeting was important, and he needed to focus. *Yes.* Focus on work, not on how red El's cheeks had gotten when he was embarrassed. The blush had spread over his face, giving him a pretty rose color.

Nope. That was a thought for later.

The conference room's lights were on when he got there. He put the drawings down and spread them out.

He'd use the television too. There were a few pictures they had taken that would be useful for visuals. But first, he needed some coffee.

"I'm bringing them back now." Sara Jo's voice filled the room.

The good old conference phone. If he'd jumped at her voice, there was no one to tell on him. He got the coffee and stood by his chair, waiting. He welcomed everyone as the group filed in and settled into their chairs. It was now or never. *Time to shine.*

Sara Jo appeared and got them drinks so he could deal with the start of the meeting. He turned the television on and a picture of the abandoned hotel as it was now above the theater filled the screen. It was a beauty, but if he had his way, the place would shine when he was done with it — and it would be an asset to Fort Wayne, something they needed. The history of the area was great, and something like the apartments they'd complete would draw people to the downtown, especially with the theater attached. Thoughts of El moved to the back of his mind and he reveled in the art of the deal.

* * * *

Two hours later and he was starving. The meeting had gone well, better than he'd anticipated. He had to get some numbers together. He wasn't sure how much the steel would be in this political climate. If there were too many tariffs, it could rack up prices and cause his bid to be too high. If only they had their own steel mill. It would help offset some of the costs. Not all of them, of course, but using their own material would help the bidding process.

That was next on his list. He had too many things hanging in the air. He took his drawings back to his office, so he could note the changes. It was going to be a long night. He wanted to get his pricing together for the first stage of the project. It was a big undertaking, one of the reasons he was making it his baby and detailing it himself. He'd just given the engineering department what they needed for the bridge project at the college and the two hospital projects they were working.

It was good to be busy. He really wished he could have given El his overtime, but the rules where there for a reason. A person could burn out working too much and they couldn't afford a safety issue. Sure, they checked and triple-checked, but things could happen. Not too long ago a tower had caused a couple deaths. Not one of their projects, thank heaven, but it made everyone in the industry more careful.

Remi settled behind his drawing table, the blueprints in front of him. He started in one corner, looking to see the dimensions on the beams for the first floor. He'd need to make sure they were correct. Sometimes the customer would ask for product that wasn't available. Just because a book said a beam was available didn't mean they were made anymore. He'd have to check with the mill. There were a couple of companies they used. He'd let the receptionist deal with that. She'd let him know if they could get it or not.

His highlighter had run out when there was a knock on the door.

"Come in." Remi looked at the clock.

Damn, it was later than he thought. He was going to have to wrap it up, because he had dinner with his dad later and that made him think of El and his proposition.

And speak of the devil… El walked into his office and shut the door behind him. He looked tired.

"Mr. Marlow —"

"Please, it's after hours. Call me Remi."

El cleared his throat. "Okay…Remi." He let out a sigh.

"You're free to talk here. Anything you say stays between us. And I've already told you that no answer is the wrong one. If you don't want to do this, I completely understand. It was a spur-of-the-moment decision on my part after a conversation with my father. He wants me to settle down. I'm not ready, but — that's beside the point. It was wrong of me to ask. You're a great asset to the company. I don't want you to think of it as a bribe or anything. It was all on the up-and-up. I promise."

"I'll do it!" El blurted out. He looked confused, like he hadn't expected to say the words.

"You…will? Wonderful!"

Now what was he going to do. He hadn't planned that far ahead.

"Yes. I had to talk to my mother. I live with her — not in the geek-in-the-basement kind of way, but she needs my help."

"That's great. I think the world would be a better place if more people took care of their parents. We should probably talk over the details. Why don't you take tonight to figure out what you want out of the deal. I'll do the same. If I didn't have a dinner date with my father, I'd say let's do this tonight, but how about tomorrow? Dinner?"

El took a deep breath.

He isn't going to back out now, is he? Not so soon after he agreed. Remi didn't know why this was so important to him all the sudden, but it was. His pretend boyfriend *had* to be El.

"I'll make arrangements for tomorrow. What time?"

"Why don't we order in? We can talk about it here in the office, so we don't have to worry about any interruptions. We'll get more accomplished. And I'm serious. You let me know what you need. I'll draw everything up. If you want a lawyer to look at it, I have no problem with that. I'll have mine look as well. And—" Remi didn't want to say it, but he was going to. He *had* to. If he didn't, he'd feel like the biggest piece of shit on the planet. "If you change your mind at any time, we'll rip up the contract. We'll even put a clause in there stating that. I don't want you to feel uncomfortable."

"I— Your lawyer is fine. I trust you. I've never had any reason to believe otherwise." El smiled.

It was shy upturn of his lips and it was adorable. Remi never really studied at him that closely, not until today. He had a nice build, dark hair and eyes. And when he smiled, his whole face lit up like nothing Remi had seen before.

"Great. I'm going to wrap this up and head out. I'll see you tomorrow?"

"Are you working on the apartments above the theater?" El indicated the plans.

"I am."

"I took a tour there when the news station did a story. It's a mess, but I bet we could make it shine." El ran his finger over the drawings.

"I totally agree."

"Well, good. Great. I'll just— Yes, see you tomorrow." El turned and left the office.

The door closed with a soft snick.

And now he had to deal with his dad. He couldn't tell him about El. Not yet. His father wasn't stupid. If Remi told his dad about his new boyfriend, he'd laugh at him. But he could set the stage. He was going to have to introduce the two soon if the plan was going to go smoothly. Even if it blew up in his face, he'd still pay El. It wouldn't be his fault.

God, am I really going to do this?

Chapter Four

El couldn't believe he'd just agreed to an idea he thought would never work. He was losing his mind, that was for sure. He was going to be the boss's boyfriend. Wait—*pretend* boyfriend. This could only end badly. Even though Mr. Marlow had said it wouldn't affect his job, El knew it could still blow up in his face. And what if something happened to his mom while he was off playing fake boyfriend? It would devastate him.

His mom had convinced him to contact hospice. El still hoped he could find a miracle cure, but she wasn't getting better. During the last doctor's visit, they'd been told it could be weeks, months if they were lucky. So far they hadn't been—not since the stupid disease had come back full force.

He had to pull the car over. He wasn't far from home, but the thought of one day going there and not having his mom made his heart hurt. El didn't know what he was going to do without her. She was his rock, the person he could always count on and the best mom a son could possibly have. And she'd done it by herself. His grandparents had passed away years ago, he had some other relatives who lived far away and he'd never known anyone on his dad's side. Once his mom was gone, he was it. El rubbed a hand over his chest, like that would stop the hurt. Nothing could stop the pressing pain ebbing through him.

The best thing he could do was stay with her, take some leave and stop this foolish nonsense that he could play fake boyfriend to a billionaire. Time with her was more important than money. He knew that. And if she hadn't encouraged him, he would have turned Mr. Marlow down flat.

El took a deep breath and pulled back into traffic. He had dinner to make for his mom. He hoped that when he got there she would at least have drank her broth, but the last couple of nights it had been sitting on her bedside table, untouched. She only seemed to eat if he forced it.

He pulled into the driveway and went inside. "Mom, I'm home."

She didn't answer. El put his coat over the kitchen chair and went to her room. She was sleeping. *So still.* He had to focus on her chest to be sure she was still breathing. He was afraid to check, just in case. He knew that one of these times she wouldn't wake up. He prayed for that — for her, at least. If she could go in her sleep without pain, he would be all for it. If he was tired of the pain, he knew she had to be exhausted.

"El." She turned her head and looked him. She had a small smile on her face.

"Yeah, Mom, I'm here."

"Come. Sit." She patted her bed.

He moved a chair closer to the bed. She was so frail. It hadn't always been that way. Growing up, he'd thought she was the strongest person around. Now she was skin and bones.

"I see you had some soup."

"I managed to get a bit down. It was good. You're getting better at making it."

"All thanks to you." El smiled, thinking about a time when he'd been about twelve. His mom had told him she was going to show him how to make something easy that he would be able to make when he was on his own—something warm and hardy...soup. That had been a fun day. She'd taught him so much.

"Flattery!" She cough-laughed. "Now, did you tell that boss of yours yes?"

"I did. But maybe I should take it back." El worried his lip between his teeth. He was so conflicted.

"Don't you dare. If I go, I go. We both know it's going to happen. Neither of us wants to talk about it, but we need to."

"I agree, Mom. But not tonight." El took her hand and kissed it. "Think you could eat some rice? Or more soup?"

"I'm not hungry, sweetie. Just tired." She closed her eyes then slipped back to sleep. It was scary how quick she could drop into a deep sleep. One day...she wouldn't wake up.

El closed his eyes. He wanted to cry, but if he started, he wouldn't stop. And there were still a couple things he needed to do tonight before he went to bed. His mom's bathroom needed cleaning, and he hadn't gotten to it over the weekend. She usually shuffled her way in there, and tomorrow he'd need to give her a bath. It was one of the things he'd never thought he'd ever do, but when the person he loved most needed the help, he was going to give it. He knew his mom hated it too. She wasn't one who liked to depend on anyone but herself. She'd learned the hard way when his father had left them, as a single mom working two jobs, sometimes three. She'd done it for him. He'd had his times being a snot to her, but there were good times too. A lot of them.

Dinner. He needed to eat something and figure out how he was going to finish his week. For now, he'd eat, clean the bathroom, take some trash out, do the dishes then head to bed. Maybe he'd have a clearer head in the morning — and *not* think about how hot his boss was or how much fun it would be to play house with him for real.

Those were dangerous thoughts. Remington Marlow could have whoever he wanted. He just didn't have time with all the work the company had taken on, and El was an easy choice to ask to play the role. He was there. The hard part would be making the senior Marlow believe the two were a couple. He hoped Remi had a plan for that.

He closed his mom's door behind him and headed for the kitchen. Sunday had been his day to prepare food for the week to make things run smoother, so he had a few things to pick from for dinner. He went for salad. He just wasn't that hungry. His emotional state didn't help and he wanted to keep the food down. *What does mom's favorite book character say? Something about tomorrow being another day?* Yeah, he'd go with that philosophy, because it seemed his life was about to become a soap opera anyway.

* * * *

For the first time in years, El dreaded going into work. Maybe it wasn't so much dread as anticipation and waiting for the other shoe to drop. Later that day, he was going to have dinner with Remi. If they were going to pretend to be boyfriends, he was going to have to get used to using the bosses name. It wouldn't look good if he called him 'Mr. Marlow' in front of his dad. That would be the end of the boyfriend charade before it even really started. And just how long was he supposed to pretend? There were questions he'd have to remember to ask later.

And he wasn't ready to spend time with Remi's father either, but he knew it would be soon. It had to be if they planned on pulling this off, whatever *this* was.

Dinner really wouldn't be too bad. At least this first time they were going to eat in the office, just the two of them. If he messed up, there wouldn't be anyone else to see. And what was he going to tell Sara Jo? She was going to want to know why he was hanging out with the boss. She saw them both every day. She was going to figure out something was going on. She wasn't stupid. Hopefully Remi had a plan for that—or maybe that could be one of the things they discussed. He really didn't want to lie to his best friend. She could be on their side and help them out. It wouldn't hurt to have someone helping them wade through the ins and outs of a deal straight out of a sitcom.

This is my life. How did I get here? He wanted normal, not television-ready.

He made his way to his desk without running into anyone. He was early, probably his nerves forcing him out of the house to get the day started. Coffee would help. He hadn't had time this morning to grab any.

He'd been busy getting his mom settled. She'd had a bad night, up and down most of the evening. She hadn't eaten much and what she did had ended up in the toilet. If it kept up, she was going to have to go back to the hospital. The nurse from hospice was supposed to come over the next day. He'd have to ask her what they could do, if anything.

The break room coffee pot was empty, but he'd expected that, because it looked like he was the first one in. He made the coffee and went back to his desk to start up his computer. He had to do a check on one of his fellow detailers' projects that morning and he was expecting another set of drawings later today to do the same. The reason he loved his job was because it forced him to focus. If he didn't, people could die. El could lose himself in the lines and structure of AutoCAD. He needed that today, in more ways than one. There was too much on his mind that he didn't want to think about.

People were starting to trickle in and the day was chugging along. Lunch was there before he knew it. He wanted to go home and get his mom fed, since he wasn't going to be home for dinner. As long as she ate something, it wouldn't matter if it was for lunch or dinner.

El took his coffee cup to the break room so he could rinse it out. Sara Jo was there. He really didn't want to talk to her yet, not until he'd figured out how they were going to deal with the 'pretend boyfriend' stuff.

"Hey, El. Headed home? How is Kathleen?"

"Not good, but yeah, I'm headed home. I need to get there. I'll talk to you later?" El turned to the door, not really waiting for an answer.

"Give her a kiss from me."

"Will do." El waved a hand and left.

It was a close call. He'd wanted to blurt out all that was going on. Sara Jo had been with him through everything—the first cancer scare, the remission and now it being back. It was one of the reasons she'd let him into Remi's office the previous day. She knew he needed the money. But the idea of an experimental drug was slipping away. In his mom's state, she might not be a candidate anymore. It was a fact he might have to face. It was becoming too real. Having hospice in the house wasn't going to help him hide his head in the sand about the seriousness of his mother's condition. He didn't even like to think about it, much less talk about it out loud. It was time to get real. *Tomorrow.*

Right now, he had to rush home and cook something for both of them to eat. He'd skipped breakfast and the coffee sloshed around his stomach. He really needed a sandwich, he really needed to stop putting off dealing with the inevitable and he really needed to face what was happening. He should have accepted sooner how bad it really was.

Deep breath.

No matter how upset he was, he couldn't let his mother see it. This was about her, not him. He pulled up to the house and took a few minutes to compose himself before he opened the door. He had to try to get her to drink something—even if it was just water—and hope she wouldn't throw it up. They had some medicine to help with nausea, but if the water wouldn't stay down, neither would the meds. One more deep breath and he went in. There was nowhere he didn't dread going today, but when he opened the door to his home, it was a gamble whether or not he would be walking into his worst nightmare.

Chapter Five

Remi paced his office. The day had dragged. He'd been stuck behind his desk, working on paperwork. He didn't mind it most days, but today was different, probably because of the dinner he was about to have. Sara Jo had left, none-the-wiser. If she'd thought something was up with how twitchy he'd been, she hadn't said anything. He was going to wait to order food until El got there, just in case he had any allergies Remi needed to know about. It wasn't a good way to start a first date by poisoning the guy.

But...this wasn't a date. It was a strategy meeting. They had to figure out what lines they would draw.

His place had a spare bedroom. He lived downtown in the luxury apartments that looked over the ball field. It was great going out on his balcony when they had a musical event. And he could catch part of the game as well. It was one of the benefits of where he lived when he was home, which lately hadn't been too often. The downtown area was being built up, and the only thing really missing was a grocery store. He could walk most places and he loved being in the center of everything.

The knock on the door startled him, mid-stride. He almost fell on his ass. He needed to pay more attention.

"Come in."

El walked in and shut the door behind him, not that he needed to. It was well after five on a Tuesday, so everyone had already left. There would be an odd person there occasionally, but only when they had a big project.

"Hi." El gave him a little smile before sitting in the chair across from Remi's desk.

"Hello. I didn't order anything yet. I wasn't sure if you were allergic to anything or had any dietary issues."

"Oh no, I'm not picky and don't have any allergies. I'll eat just about anything."

"Good to know. Chinese? I know an excellent place that delivers."

"That sounds great."

"What would you like?"

El thought a moment then said, "A small hot-and-sour soup, a couple of egg rolls, sweet-and-sour chicken with white rice. Oh! And some crab Rangoon."

"That sounds great. If you want to go over to the table, I'll order then we can start chatting."

Why am I nervous? This was a straightforward deal. It shouldn't have anything to do with the fact that he found El attractive. From the time he'd started at the company, it had been drilled into his head by his father to never date an employee. And…did this really count? They weren't dating for real. It was a business deal, just like any other. Only…this one would require that El be living in close quarters with him. They'd be working together and Remi had to keep it professional so he didn't lose a valued employee.

He placed the order and learned that it would be about hour before it got there. That should give them some time to get down a few details. Remi took his laptop to the sitting area where he'd directed El. It wasn't anything fancy, just a couch, a couple of chairs and a small table. That way, on nights when he needed some place other than his desk to work — or if he was eating in — he had a comfortable place. He could be at his office at all hours. His employees might have restricted overtime, but he just worked until he was finished.

The fun of being the boss.

El cleared his throat. "I think we should tell Sara Jo. I mean, she is going to figure out something is up anyway. We need her on our side. That way, she can run interference if we need her to."

"That is an excellent idea. I was wondering how we would deal with her, because I knew you were friends."

"Yeah, I don't want to lie to her. And I have to tell you that I told my mom."

"Okay. That's fine." Remi didn't know how he really felt about that, but he really didn't have a choice in the matter.

"Don't worry. It isn't like she's going to blab."

"That's okay."

I guess we're getting right down to business. He'd figured there would be a bit of small talk first, but he liked a man who knew his own mind.

"Good. Okay. Good. Um… I'm not sure why you need to get a fake boyfriend. I mean, you — Well, you could have just about anyone."

"My dad wants me to settle down. I think I told you that before. I can't remember. I just sort of blurted everything out before. But, yeah, my dad wants me settled and happy, like he was with my mom. I'm too busy with work. I really don't want a relationship. But if I show him I'm giving it a good try, I'm hoping he'll back off a little."

"That sounds... Well, it kind of sucks that he's forcing the issue."

"It does, but, my dad is old school. He's fine with me being gay, but I should be in a relationship and thinking about kids. So, that is why I propositioned you. I figured, you know the schedule, you know the work and how much goes into it and you needed the overtime. That brings us to you. Why do you need the money? We should be as up front with each other as possible."

"Bills, for the most part. I just need some extra time. To tell you the truth, I'm just not sure I can leave my mom alone. She said to agree to this so...I am."

"Fair enough. We should talk about a time frame. I'm thinking a couple months should do it, maybe three with the option of longer. I figure we can do dinner with my dad this weekend, maybe. I can drop some hints this week. We can move you in—maybe in a couple weeks? I don't want to rush it or he'll get suspicious."

"He won't think it's odd that he talked to you about settling down and now you have a boyfriend?"

"I don't think so, not if I play it right. I mean...you work here. He's told me not to fish in my own pond, but hopefully he'll just think our attraction was too great. Yes, I know, that sounds odd, but it's his way." Remi laughed.

"I can see that. Okay, so…three months with an option for more. I move in sometime not too long after we've had dinner with your dad. Would you really move someone in that fast?"

"Probably not, but we've known each other for a while, so it's different."

"Not really. We've worked together, but how well do we really know each other? I mean, I know you own the company. I know what the business plans are, thanks to Sara Jo's emails. We've chatted at a company picnic or two, but we've never sat down and really talked."

"Guess that will change, won't it? If nothing else comes out of this, maybe we could be friends. You can't have too many of those. Winter is coming, so business will slow down a bit soon. Maybe, after this experience, we'll be closer and each have a new buddy to go out with when we have time. Well…maybe you already have time."

Remi was rambling. *Why is this so hard?*

But he kept right on talking. "We should probably find out about each other's likes and stuff. I think the legal stuff is primarily the length of time and stating that you'll have your own room in the apartment. But I guess we should talk about money."

"God, I really hate this. Maybe I should just do it as a favor," El offered.

"No. You need some extra cash. Maybe we should look at what you make now and go from there. Use your overtime pay amount and calculate the duration of the contract to come up with a figure." Remi clicked a few keys on his nearby laptop to get to payroll. He didn't run it himself but had access to it.

Wow, we aren't paying him enough. At least he wasn't on salary and could make a bit more with overtime. Remi didn't want to make an outrageous offer, but he didn't want to lowball it either.

"How about fifteen thousand dollars? If I set it up as a gift, then it won't be taxed. That is the max amount allowed."

"That is— I can't— Wow. I think that might be too much."

"I don't think so. You're worth it and you're helping me out. Would it help?"

"Yes. But I feel like I'm taking money for nothing. I mean, all I'm going to do is move in with you and pretend to be your boyfriend. Nothing will really change much. And part of that time I won't even be living with you. I mean, I guess I could cook for us or clean up your place. Free money... It just seems too good to be true."

"I have a maid that comes in once a week. And, if you want to cook, you totally can. I have a great kitchen that doesn't get enough use."

"Okay. Well, maybe I could cook for you and your dad for our dinner? How would that be? It would make me feel better to be doing something. That is way more than I would get for a few hours of overtime and you know it."

"It's settled. And I think the idea of a dinner at my apartment is great. He'd like that. I'll arrange it. Just let me know what you want to cook, and I'll have everything you need. Is there anything else you think we should talk about? Our food should almost be here. You have plenty of time to think of things while we eat."

El was thoughtful. "We have the amount and the time span, and we've already discussed me being able to cancel whenever I want. I'm not sure what else we'll need in a contract. It isn't like I've ever done anything like this before. It could be open-ended, so if we think of something we can add it in. I really don't need a full contract anyway. I trust you. If I didn't, I wouldn't be working here. I like it because the people are great and that includes the higher-ups. You have always treated us right. That goes a long way." El held out his hand.

Remi shook it. He couldn't believe his luck that he'd come across El when he had. It all could have gone much worse.

There was a buzzing sound coming from his computer. He looked down to see that the front door had been locked and the delivery driver was trying to get in.

"That would be our food. Let me get it." He jumped off the couch, put his laptop down and headed for the door. He left the office door open this time. The building was quiet. No one was around except the two of them.

After he paid the delivery man and was headed back to his office, he thought about where he was. He loved walking through the building when no one was there. He enjoyed the fact that this was his. He'd helped build it to what it was today. He was proud of his company, and it had warmed his heart to hear all the good things El had had to say. Remi just did what he believed was proper, and he was going to do right by El. He made that vow to himself then and there. If anything, they would end friends. He wasn't lying when he'd said a person couldn't have too many. He only had a very few and El would be welcome anytime. His stomach growled.

Time to eat.

Chapter Six

Well, it was going better than expected. El rubbed his sweaty palms down his pants to dry them. He hadn't tripped over his words and he'd gotten it out right away that he wanted Sara Jo in on the deal. He really needed someone in his corner. With his mom going downhill fast, he was afraid he'd fall apart. Should he tell Remi about what was happening at home? He just wasn't sure it was something his boss really needed to know, at least not yet. It wasn't affecting his work, and he'd only asked for overtime. He decided that if it was going to start messing with his job, he'd say something then.

Remi didn't take long to get back with the food. It smelled wonderful and he was ready to eat. El didn't realize how hungry he'd gotten. Most of the time he was more worried about getting food into his mom, not himself.

"Do you use chopsticks or a fork?" Remi set the bags on the floor before he sat down and started pulling things out.

"Fork. I never could figure out how to use chopsticks. My mom can do it, no problem, but I just can't." El didn't let himself get choked up about the thought of his mom. It wasn't the time.

"I would totally impress you with my chopstick skills, but I can't use them either." Remi shrugged and laughed.

He had a great laugh and it went straight to El's dick. *That* could be embarrassing.

Not a date. Not a date.

No matter how many times he thought the words, it felt like date. They were talking and eating. But what did he know? He hadn't been on a date for a really long time.

"Equal footing... I like that." El smiled.

Remi handed him his egg rolls, crab Rangoon and hot and sour soup, along with some utensils. His stomach might have growled, but he ignored it.

"It smells good. Here." Remi passed him the sweet-and-sour chicken. "Dig in. It smells so good. I didn't realize how ravenous I was."

"Me either."

They ate in silence for a while to take an edge off their hunger. The food was better than El had expected. He hadn't had Chinese food this good...ever. He'd have to ask for the name of the restaurant. Maybe his mom would eat some soup from there.

"I do have a question." El put his fork down.

"Shoot." Remi shoved a few noodles into his mouth.

"How should we act at work? I mean, we're supposed to be a couple for your dad. He does come here. Not often, but if he's here — "

Remi set his box down on the table, giving El all his focus. "I think we should act like we always do. I mean, we *are* at work. So, we'd be professional, no matter what. Right?"

"Yes. You're right." El nodded.

"And if my father comes here and would want to see you, I can always call you into the office. I don't think he'd bother you in *your* office. We can play it by ear. You'll know more after you meet him. And I don't think the interaction between the two of you would make anyone think we were a couple."

"That makes me feel better. I don't want people to think I'm sleeping my way to the top." El chuckled, but it was a bit awkward. It was something he'd worried about, dating the boss.

Remi laughed as well. "We don't have to worry about that. Even if we were dating for real, it wouldn't interfere with our duties. You're a hard worker. You're one of the best in the company. Others already look to you for advice."

"Well…" El's face heated up. Damn it, he just knew he was blushing.

"Don't be embarrassed, El. It's the truth. One of the reasons I wanted to draw up a contract was so you'd feel comfortable. I don't want to lose you as a valuable employee. You're an asset to the company, as I'm sure your supervisor has told you. Plus, you don't directly work for me. Sure, I'm the big boss, but you have a supervisor who overseas your day-to-day work."

"All that is very true. Good, that makes me feel better." El went back to eating his soup.

Knowing where he stood helped him feel more comfortable about the whole situation. And, at least he wasn't moving into Remi's apartment right off the bat. They could schedule stuff and he could be home with his mom at night.

"I'm happy I can make you feel comfortable. Thank you for agreeing to this ridiculous idea. We might just pull it off."

"I hope so. That way you don't have to worry about your dad pushing someone on you that you don't want." El couldn't imagine someone telling him he'd better settle down or else.

He didn't know the elder Mr. Marlow that well, but he didn't seem like the type of guy who would push. Maybe there was more involved than Remi was letting on.

There was a knock at the door and who should walk in but the senior Marlow. *This isn't awkward at all.* El didn't think they'd been overheard.

"Dad! What are you doing here?" Remi stood.

"Sorry. You weren't answering your phone. I didn't mean to interrupt..." Jackson Marlow looked between the two of them.

It would look like a date. And...that seemed to fall right into their plan. El decided to roll with it. It was, after all, what Remi was going to be paying him for.

"Hello, Mr. Marlow. Sorry. I don't think we wanted you to find out this way." El walked forward and held out his hand.

"Find out?" A grin spread across his face.

"Dad—" Remi looked a little confused for a second.

"It's okay, Remi. It was bound to come out." El shrugged.

"Son, I thought you weren't dating."

"You know who Elros is, don't you?" Remi asked.

"I do. He is one of the detailers in the company."

"Right. And what have you told me time and time again?"

"Don't fish in your own pond. But, you're older now. As long as it doesn't interfere with work, I don't see it as an issue. Why did you throw such a fit yesterday?" Mr. Marlow frowned.

"Because I was fishing in my own pond and I didn't want you to know." Remi shook his head.

The phrase was a tad ridiculous. El would have shaken his head in sympathy if he wasn't worried about impressing Remi's dad.

"We were just talking about dinner this weekend. I was going to cook for Remi. If you want to come over...?" El offered.

"If you two don't mind, I'd really like that." Jackson was still smiling.

"Good. Remi, I'm going to leave. I need to get home, but I'll see you tomorrow." El took a bold step and walked to Remi to buss his cheek with a kiss.

They were supposed to be boyfriends, so it seemed the natural thing to do.

"You don't have to leave on my account," Mr. Marlow assured him.

"It's okay. It's getting late and I have an early start in the morning." El held out his hand again for another handshake.

"I'll walk you out." Remi smiled.

They held hands until they were at El's car. He was just happy his palms weren't sweaty. That would have been gross.

"That was—"

"Too much?" El worried his lip.

"No...genius. I would have never thought to start now. And I was thrown that my dad was there and we'd just been talking about him. Wow, you can really think on your feet!" Remi pulled him in for a hug.

Their bodies were flush against each other and El needed to take a few deep breaths, which was a bad idea because Remi smelled so good. The nearness was over almost as soon as it had begun, but it was enough for El to dream about later. God, he was so stupid — or maybe horny. It didn't matter. This was all fake. Maybe not the hug, but…everything else. He'd say it as many times as he needed to so he'd get it through his thick skull. He and Remi were *never* going to be a thing. *We're from different worlds.*

"I'm happy it worked. I just thought, *He's here. Let's start this.* I know you were going to ease him in, but this way, you don't have to and it seems more natural." El shrugged like it was no big thing.

"I totally agree. And the way you just threw dinner out there too? Yeah, brilliant." Remi grinned.

"Thanks. Well, see you tomorrow." El waved before turning to get into his car.

"How about lunch?"

"I can't. I mean, I'd like to, you know, but I go to see my mom during my lunch. She needs me."

"Well, we can talk a bit before you leave tomorrow to get dinner with my dad planned out. How does that sound?"

El was grateful that Remi hadn't asked why he had to take care of his mom. El wasn't ready to talk about her with Remi — not in detail, not yet.

"Great. I'll think about what I want to make, probably something simple. I'm an okay cook, so it won't be anything fancy."

"It'll just be nice to eat something that isn't fast food. So, thank you for that too. See you tomorrow."

Remi shut his door for him and headed back to the office. El put his head on the steering wheel. It was going to be a long three months and he was hoping they didn't have to extend things. Remi had been a crush, and now he was going to be seeing a lot of him. Hell, living with him for a bit. It was not going to be good for his libido, for sure.

The drive home didn't take as long as usual because he was lost in thought and on autopilot. The house was just like he'd left it. He put his things away before going to his mom's room. She was asleep. The cup of broth he'd given her earlier was still full, sitting on her bed stand. He was going to have to face the hard truth…soon. His mother was going to die. It was going to happen before he was ready.

El took the broth out of the room and dumped it down the sink. Tomorrow he would meet with the hospice nurse. She was going to be there at lunchtime and she planned to stay for a bit. Maybe she could get his mom to eat something. He just knew that he didn't want his mother back in the hospital, especially not if she was going to leave him. He wanted her to be comfortable in her own home for whatever time she had left.

He sat down at the table, the food from dinner gurgling in his stomach. He wanted to cry but was afraid to start, afraid he would never stop. Shaking his head at the hopelessness of the situation, El stood to wash the lunch dishes then he tidied up the kitchen before taking a shower and going to bed. It was all too much.

He couldn't rest. The more he thought about life without his mom, the worse he felt. He sat up in bed with a start then rushed to the bathroom. Dinner didn't taste as good coming back up. He heaved until nothing more would come out then turned on the water, cupped his hand under it, sipped a bit to swirl around in his mouth then spit it out. He did that a couple of times before taking a drink.

It was going to be a long night. He lay awake thinking about the future. Tomorrow was going to be hell. The rest of his life would be too, when he lost the only person who had ever loved him, no matter what. *How does someone live without their heart?* He knew people who did, but it just didn't seem possible, none of it.

But tomorrow he would put on his brave face. He would get his mom ready for the day, meet the nurse and talk to Remi about the weekend. It seemed like he was abandoning his mom. His head knew that wasn't true, but his heart was having a hard time with it.

She was the one who had told him to do this, so he was doing it to satisfy her.

For her.

He finally drifted off to sleep again, still thinking about what he was doing for her—living for her, dreaming her dreams.

Chapter Seven

"So, you *are* dating." Jackson grinned.

"Dad—"

Remi wasn't going to live this down. He'd never thought about that part of the plan, the gloating that his father would do about being right. He was surprised his dad wasn't doing a happy dance.

He'd just come back from walking El to his car. Remi had felt the urge to kiss his pretend boyfriend, but he'd refrained. He'd experienced a bit of disappointment when El had declined his invitation to lunch. He rubbed his chest. It was...odd, to say the least. Why had it felt like a real date, despite the talk of contracts and a fake relationship?

He didn't want a relationship. He didn't have time for one. The big apartment job above the theater was a step away from being green lit. Plus, he had another project he was eyeing. There was a building across town that would be perfect for low-cost housing. If they got the theater apartment project, he could afford to put more money back into the community to help people who needed a place to live but didn't have the funds. It was something he'd been looking into for a long time now. He'd own the property, do the designs and hire a company to fill it up. It was a side project that he hadn't even told his dad about yet. It was almost time to let him in on it, but right now, his father was beaming over what he'd thought was a date.

El had been quick on his feet, for sure. Remi would have never thought to use the situation to his advantage. The truth was, he'd been stunned when his dad had shown up and he'd frozen.

He moved over to the table and started putting stuff away. He'd have to give El his leftovers the next day.

"I just don't understand why you gave me a hard time about wanting you settled."

"It's new, Dad, and I didn't like the fact that you were trying to push something on me when I might not be ready for it. Can you understand that?"

Remi moved to the mini fridge in the corner of his office and moved things around so he could get the Chinese food put away.

"Remi, I know you don't understand. Maybe when you're older and you're looking back on your life, you'll figure it out. I'm old. There are no guarantees in this world, and before something happens to me, I want you taken care of. I don't want you to be lonely."

"It isn't like I don't have other family, Dad, plus you're not going anywhere any time soon. You're too stubborn to leave this world." He turned toward his father.

"You have me there, but I am older, and it's just been you and me for so long. I know you have cousins, aunts and uncles, but it isn't the same. You aren't close to them, and you know that if something happens to me, you'll most likely lose touch. You'll probably stay here at the office and work yourself to death. I want more than that for you."

"Okay, Dad, you're right. Happy?" Remi threw up his hands in exasperation.

"I am now. And I can't believe your young man invited me for dinner—and at your place, no less. I didn't think you ever used the kitchen."

"You're a funny man. I've cooked in it. It's just been a while. Now, why did you really stop by?"

"I told you… You weren't answering your phone. Of course, now I know why, and if you would have told me about Elros, I wouldn't have interrupted."

"It's okay and I'm sorry about that. The mainline goes right to voicemail after five and my phone is on vibrate. He wasn't going to stay much longer anyway. We have work tomorrow. He's doing some checking on parts of the apartment drawings."

"How is that coming?"

"It's coming. I'll have a quote for them sometime tomorrow. They made it sound like a done deal. I'll feel better after we get everything signed and ready to go. We can break ground soon."

"Good. I've been in that old building and can't wait to see what you have planned."

"It's going to be spectacular. I might even want to move."

"That's saying something, my boy. I know how much you love looking over the ball field."

"I do, but these apartments have history. And I'd be right there by the Embassy Theater for plays and such."

"That reminds me. I have tickets to something happening on Friday night. I'll have to see. It's part of my season pass. Do you want to take Elros?"

"That's okay, Dad. You go. I know how much you enjoy going there. I think there was something going on at the War Memorial Coliseum this weekend. The farm and garden show, maybe? I wanted to take a look before heading to the farmers' market at the ball field."

"What time do I need to be over on Saturday for dinner?"

"Let me talk to Elros, and I'll get back to you."

"Sounds good." Jackson hugged Remi before leaving.

This is a bad idea. He knew it. He really did. So why was he going ahead with it and looking forward to seeing El the next day? He shook his head before gathering his computer and coat. Thankfully, his dad hadn't looked at the computer, because it had contract information about his fake relationship.

The food had been packed away, his desk was clean as it could be and he had to leave before he started working on the bid for the complex. If he began to do that, he wouldn't leave the office.

He needed to get home and take a shower, to wash the day away and maybe think more about this whole situation. Would it be so wrong to really date El? They had things in common. He liked El more than he'd thought he would.

Remi shook his head. Enough thoughts of that. He locked up the building and headed for his car. There was a bit of a chill in the air, but it felt good. He was looking forward to a night in his bed. The previous night he *had* stayed at the office and the couch had been comfortable, but it wasn't his bed. Remi loved his space and he wanted to spend more time there. He vowed to take some time off once the apartment deal was off his desk and in the bag.

Downtown Fort Wayne was pretty at night with the lights shining. Driving around the city really relaxed him. Sometimes he forgot how beautiful it could be at night. When there weren't clouds, the stars were so bright in the sky, like tonight. Maybe he'd grab a beer and sit on his balcony tonight before bed. It really wasn't that late.

Parking wasn't the best downtown, but he had a space he rented in a parking garage that was close to his place. It was attached to a sports bar-restaurant. It was convenient enough, unless it was a game day. On those occasions, he was extra lucky to have a spot, because the search for parking got frantic.

He grabbed his laptop, locked his car and headed up. The brisk night air was refreshing and enough to wake him up a bit. He opened his door and stepped into his space. He looked around it with fresh eyes, trying to decide what El would think when he saw it. The walls were light taupe. Usually decor was white, but he loved that his felt warm when he walked in. There were a few pictures hanging on the walls, but it was minimal. The best thing about it, other than the ball field outside his back door, was the comfortable couch and the big-screen television. That was where he spent the nights he had off. Sometimes he liked to lounge with Netflix on in the background. That reminded him… There was a new show he wanted to catch — some original thing people were talking about.

But first he needed to get out of his suit into a nice pair of sweats with a sweatshirt. The bedroom consisted of a California king bed and not much else. He had an end table and a television mounted to his wall. If he wasn't on his couch, he was in his bedroom. He liked to fall asleep to the television. There was also a gaming system attached to this one. It was his guilty pleasure, but he wasn't about that tonight. Nope, he wanted fresh air and the stars—and maybe a new Netflix show later.

He changed quickly, putting his clothes away before swinging by his kitchen, grabbing a beer and heading outside. The view was spectacular. The ball field was dark. There was no game or people milling about, just the quiet of the night. Well, mostly quiet... The people next door had some music playing just loud enough that Remi could hear it but not make out the words. From the other side, the smell of something cooking wafted over to him.

The life of an apartment dweller wasn't for everyone, but he loved it and wouldn't have it any other way. There was no yard to worry about, no snow to shovel in the winter. If he had a problem, he called management. *I'm living the life.*

The stars shined brightly, and he thought about El. *Am I doing the guy wrong? Can I really expect this to go smoothly? What will happen in a couple of months when this is over? What if El gets attached? Hell, what if I get attached?* He was already feeling something—probably lust, but it was there, a feeling he hadn't had in years. *Shit.* He couldn't remember the last real boyfriend he'd had except for Harry. Maybe that was where all the emotion was coming from, the fact that his hand had been his best friend for months. Time would tell, but by then, would it be too late? He didn't want to hurt El. He didn't want to hurt his dad, but if he wasn't careful, it could happen. He knew it.

It will just have to work. El needed the money and Remi couldn't take that opportunity away from him. Of course, he was the boss. He could just okay the overtime and call it a day, but there was something about El he needed to know more about. Maybe he hadn't noticed it before. It wasn't a bad thing, he supposed, that his attention was drawn to a person when it might not have been if not for his dad's interference. Maybe he should thank his father for that.

They could be friends. There was nothing that said just because they were two gay men living together that they had to sleep together. There could be no attraction on El's side. That would be a good thing and make things go smoother. If Remi's cock demanded attention, he was going to ignore it.

The best thing he could do right now was enjoy the night and his beer. He took a drink and sighed. First world problems at their finest. It was too late to worry about what should have been, what he should have said. Things were moving forward. He needed to think about dinner—and decide exactly when El should move in.

Remi didn't want to move too fast. His father might be happy right now, but the minute he suspected something was off, he'd figure out the plan. His dad was a lot of things, but stupid wasn't one of them. Remi loved his dad something fierce. When his mom had died, he'd thought he'd lose his dad too. He'd pulled his dad out of a depression and together they'd survived his mother's death. This was the least he could do for the old man. When he 'broke up' with El, he'd take comfort from his dad and tell him it simply wasn't meant to be, that it was just the two of them against the world.

He wondered why that made him so sad. Remi leaned back in his chair and looked out at the night, ignoring the loneliness he didn't want to admit feeling. He was fine by himself. He always had been.

Chapter Eight

Morning appeared way too early. El hadn't slept very well. He'd tossed and turned and thought about what was going to happen that weekend when he went to Remi's and had to cook dinner. But even before that, he was going to have to meet with the hospice nurse. He wasn't looking forward to any of it, truth be told. It was going to wreck him. He'd rather stay home, taking care of his mom like she'd taken care of him for years.

She hadn't slept well either. She was in too much pain and he could hear her from his room. He'd gotten up during the night and asked her if she wanted to go to the ER, but she'd refused.

His life seemed to be spinning out of control. The only constant was his work. That he could do. It didn't get sick and die. It didn't try to date him. He used the programs, checked the specs and did his job so no one got hurt. That was what he did and he was good at it.

Today he was working on the big apartment deal that everyone was talking about. He needed to print up a list of metals needed for his section, so they could get quotes and Remi could place the bid. A couple of the other guys in the department were working on different sections. Once he got his done, he'd pass it on for someone to check and he'd check another person's. Remi would do the ultimate check and finalize the bid for the company.

It was noon before he realized it. He had to hurry up if he was going to meet with the nurse. The plan was for her to stay there for the rest of the day and set up a routine. As much as he didn't want the distance between him and his mom, he was run down from taking care of her and trying to keep her out of the hospital.

"El."

He was putting on his coat and turned when he heard his name. Remi was at the office door.

"Hey, Remi. I'm just heading out."

"Okay. That's good. Um…I have your leftovers upstairs whenever you want them."

"Oh! You didn't have to do that."

"It wasn't any problem." Remi smiled.

His smile is beautiful. He should smile more. It made his whole face light up. El wasn't used to being on the receiving end of something so spectacular. *And now I'm being silly.*

"Okay, after work? I can come to your office." El finished buttoning his coat.

Remi put his hands in his pockets and rocked back on his heels.

"Wonderful." Remi hesitated for a minute, like he wanted to say something more, but he didn't.

El might have asked him what he needed, but he was too in his head about his mom.

The drive home seemed to take forever today. Impending doom filled his chest.

There was a car in the driveway when he got there. It had to be the nurse but she wasn't in the car. Could his mom have even gotten up to let her in?

Now that he'd thought about it, there was a danger every day that he left her by herself. What had he been thinking? He should have stopped working, taken family leave. El started panting, his chest tight. He was having a panic attack. He rushed into the house, only to see his mom sitting in her chair. When was the last time he'd seen that? *Months.* He stopped in front of her and the strange man standing over her.

"Hello. You must be Elros. I'm Brett, your mother's new nurse." He held out a hand.

"Yes, hello." He looked between his mom and the guy.

Why he'd expected a woman, he didn't know. El's breathing returned to normal. Today wasn't the day he was going to lose her.

"I was just talking to Kathleen. She's been telling me all about you and how much you do for her."

"Well—"

"I'm here to help. You don't need to worry, okay? She's in good hands." Brett smiled.

It was too bright and didn't belong in the house, but somehow it did make El feel a bit better.

"El, why don't you go get some lunch? Eat before you go back to work." His mom spoke softly. He had to strain to hear her. She looked tired and he hated it.

"Do you want some broth?"

"No. I'm going to go back to bed in a moment. I just wanted to be up when you met Brett."

"Let me help you." El moved closer.

"No. No. Go eat. Relax for a change." She waved him away.

"I'll take her to bed and meet you in the kitchen." Brett was still smiling.

He wasn't going to like what Brett was going to say. He might be smiling, but he had sad eyes. El did an about-face and went to the kitchen. He wasn't hungry now, but he knew that if he didn't eat something, he'd be starving by the end of the day and that would take away focus from his job.

There were a couple of pre-made meals, but he decided he'd like a sandwich. He pulled out the fixings and waited for the voice of doom to come meet him for a talk.

"Sorry that I just came right into the house. I wasn't sure if you'd be here or not."

"That's okay. I'm surprised she was able to let you in. She doesn't get around too well." El concentrated on his sandwich.

"I think she's having a good day."

The sound of a chair scraping across the floor jolted El from himself.

"Will she have many more?" he couldn't help but ask. El closed his eyes. He didn't want to hear what the nurse was going to say, but he had to know.

"Maybe? The nice thing is that I can keep her comfortable. I have access to drugs that only a medical professional can administer. I'm just happy you called us when you did."

"How much longer?"

"It's hard to say. I'm not a doctor."

"No, you aren't, but you been doing this for a while, haven't you?"

"Yes, I have. I'm sorry."

Elros sighed. "I'm not ready."

"I'm here for you too, you know."

"Just keep her comfortable for as long as she has. She doesn't want to die in a hospital."

"Most people don't. I'll be here and help her, look after her."

"I should be here."

"You've done an excellent job so far, but you need the help. You have a life to live. You can't do this on your own and your mother will rest better if she knows you are living it."

"I was in denial." Elros didn't want to say more. He was afraid he'd start crying any minute and he needed to get back to work. Just thinking about it made him feel like shit. Sure, he came home for lunch every day and he was there every night, but it wasn't enough. All the minutes counted now.

"There's nothing wrong with that. I'm here to ease some of the burden. I gave her a little something for the pain, so she should sleep for a few hours. She needs the rest. She told me she's had a hard time sleeping because of the pain."

"Yeah, the last couple of nights have been bad. I'm going to go say goodbye before I head back to work. You'll be here when I get home?"

"Yes, I'll be here until around six."

El gave a small nod and left the kitchen. He left the remains of his sandwich on the table, needing to see his mom more than he needed to eat—at least to assure himself she was okay for now.

She turned her head when he entered the room. There was a smile on her face and she didn't appear to be in pain.

"Hey, baby... You headed back to work?"

"I should stay," El insisted.

"No, you shouldn't. This disease shouldn't be allowed to kill both of us. Promise me you'll live and not shut down when I'm gone."

"Mom…"

"You promise me right now."

"I love you."

"I love you too, Elros. I would give anything to stay with you longer. I know you're going to hurt when I'm gone, but *live*. Do the things I never could."

"I promise, Mom." El leaned over and kissed her forehead.

"That's my boy. Now, tell me about your dinner."

"It was nice. He's a great guy, Mom. He's doing this for his dad. I'm going to cook dinner for them this weekend. It should be…interesting."

"Are you still moving in?"

"Not yet. We're going to take it slow. If I moved in tomorrow, his dad would wonder what was going on, why we were moving so fast. We're playing things by ear right now. Dinner will be the start of it all. His dad showed up last night while we were having dinner."

"That is so nice. I wish…"

She'd fallen asleep mid-sentence.

I wish too, Mom.

Elros kissed her again before leaving. He swung by the kitchen. Brett was still there. He threw the left-over sandwich into the trash. He'd had enough, and his stomach was already in a knot. He couldn't possibly eat anything more.

"There's some coffee in the cupboard. Help yourself to anything. She's asleep right now. I'm going to head back to work."

"I'll take you up on the coffee."

"Thanks again." Elros gave him a small smile and left.

On the drive back to work, he managed to get a hold of himself. His mom wasn't dead yet. Tonight he'd put on her favorite movie, watch it with her and find out what she wanted to do in the next few days. For now, he'd compartmentalize everything. If he didn't, he'd be a mess — and he'd promised his mom he'd move on somehow.

The day passed fast once he'd dug into work. It was five o'clock before he knew it. He turned off his computer and grabbed his coat. He was supposed to see Remington before he left. There was leftover Chinese food to pick up. Maybe his mom would want some. It wasn't her favorite, but she enjoyed it every now and again. She'd probably say no, though he'd try the soup on her. Broth was about all she could keep down.

Sara Jo had already left before he got there. He knocked on Remington's door frame, because the door wasn't shut.

"Hey, Elros. Come on in."

"I'm about to head out."

"I'll walk you to your car. I'm headed home as well. There's nothing left to do except wait on the downtown apartments. Hopefully we'll know something tomorrow. I have your food right here."

"You really didn't have to save it."

"It's the least I could do. Did you think about what you're going to make this weekend? I can run by the store and pick things up for you."

Elros hadn't thought about *what* he was going to make, just that he was going to make something. *What can I pull off without too much worry?*

"Um...tacos? he finally decided. "That seems easy and fun. We'd just need meat, cheese, beans, lettuce, salsa, cream cheese, the spices and taco shells."

"Mm-m, now I'm hungry." Remington rubbed his stomach.

Elros laughed. He'd needed that. The interaction was normal and not awkward at all.

"I like that sound." Remington winked.

"What sound?" Elros frowned.

"Your laugh. It's great. You seem a little sad, though. Is everything okay?"

"Yeah, just...things. You know."

Remington nodded. "I'll just grab this." He took the food out of a mini fridge that Elros hadn't noticed the previous night. He looked around the office. It was really nice, much roomier than his. But he was just lucky he had his own office. Years before, all the detailers had been shoved into one big room until the company had done their expansion."

"Thanks. Dinner tonight." Elros took the containers.

For this brief minute, he didn't worry about his mom or about the fake dating. He was enjoying Remington's presence and was at peace. Would it last? Probably not, but he was going to take his feelings right now as a win.

They walked out of the building together. There were no cars in the parking lot except theirs. Remington locked up and actually walked Elros all the way to his car. *Like last night.* They stared at each other for a few minutes. Elros wanted to lean in and see what Remington tasted like, but a car horn in the distance shook him out of that thought. They were faking it. That meant no kisses.

"Night." Elros opened his door and put the food on the passenger seat then got in and buckled up.

Remington gave a small nod and shut the door before walking to his own vehicle. It was for the best—the non-kiss. His moment of peace was gone, but he wouldn't soon forget it.

Chapter Nine

Before Remington knew it, Saturday had arrived — the day El was going to cook tacos at his place. Had it only been a week since he'd asked El to be his pretend boyfriend? It seemed much longer. They hadn't had much interaction for the last few days. He'd been tied up with the apartment project. They'd gotten the bid and would start work as soon as possible. All the drawings would have to be approved by the architect, but once that happened, they would get the green light to get their hands dirty.

First there would be a crew inside to gut the place. Then the Marlow team would start the build with the metal. Tonight wasn't only about convincing his dad he was ready to settle down, but it was also a celebration. He also planned to also tell his dad about the low-income housing project he was going to sink some money into.

All and all, it should be a good night. *So, why am I nervous?* It was all business.

El was due to show up at any time to start cooking. Remington wanted to give him a tour of the place before his dad got there so El could become more comfortable in the space. They were supposed to have been dating for longer than a week, and if they had been, El would have been to the apartment enough to know where stuff was at.

Remington paced back and forth. He was being silly. He should watch some television while he waited — or read some of the book he'd started a month ago and had never finished. He wanted to do something to take his mind off what the evening could bring.

The buzzer sounded. El was there. Remington hurried to the door and pushed the button.

"Yes."

"Um…hello. It's El."

Remington buzzed him in.

Stop being stupid. Not a date. Business only. I've got this.

It was just a simple evening in. They'd have dinner, probably talk shop. It would just be a friendly night — with his dad and a man he'd found he was attracted to. That was the bitch of the situation. He wasn't supposed to feel anything. They could be friends — or at least friendly — but romantically, sexually? Remington didn't want that. *Or do I?* Who was he trying to convince?

The knock on his door startled him. It shouldn't have. He *knew* El was on the way up.

Get a hold of yourself.

Remington opened the door and had to smile.

El looked a tad rumpled, with his jacket falling off his shoulders. His hair was a mess, like he'd run his fingers through it a few times. If he had one word for El right then, it would have been 'adorable'.

"I brought some Corona and limes. I hope that's okay. I figured it'd go well with the tacos." El held out the six-pack.

"Excellent." Remi took it from him. "Come on in. I'll take the beer and put it in the fridge. Make yourself at home. If you want to hang your coat up, the closet is to the right."

"Right. Okay."

El was nervous too. That made Remi feel a bit better. It was nice not to be the only one who wasn't sure about the whole situation. They hadn't even gotten around to signing the contract. He needed to take care of that to remind himself that this wasn't personal.

He put the beer in the fridge then turned to see El standing at the counter that separated the kitchen from the living room. He loved the open floor plan of his apartment. He could look into his dining slash living room from the kitchen. The television was actually situated so he could see it if he happened to cook, which really didn't happen often.

"I figured I'd show you around before you start cooking. And I can help you. Dad isn't supposed to be here until later, so that gives us plenty of time. We can start in an hour or so. I wanted to let you get comfortable with the place, though I know it isn't a lot of time. I wish we would have had a chance to meet here before now."

"We've been busy." El shrugged.

It was nice to finally meet someone who understood that his work was important. Of course, they did work together, so El knew what went into the company, as opposed to some guy he'd met in a bar.

"We have. It should slow down a little now that the project is near to being greenlit," Remi noted.

"I enjoy the rush. Staying busy makes the day go faster. Plus, we've had a few smaller projects. We had this guy come to the sales office and ask us to make a base for these wood tables he does. They are beautiful. They passed the project to me the other day," El said.

"I saw that. I took a break and walked around the shop. I can't wait to see the finished product."

"I was impressed. It'll be a nice mixture of wood and metal. I've seen some pictures of other projects he's done. The man is very talented."

"Okay, no more shop talk" — Remi clapped his hands together — "At least for right now. I'm sure my dad will want to talk about everything going on with the company. Let me show you around. This is the kitchen, of course, and behind you is the dining room. You walked through the living room. If we go back through there, on the other side are the two bedrooms."

Remington gestured for El to go ahead of him. They walked the short distance to the room. He tried to not get too close, but whatever scent El wore, it was tantalizing. El stopped right before the bedroom door and Remi was an inch away from running into his back. That could have been embarrassing.

"Right. Okay. Here are the two bedrooms. The master is through here and I have a bathroom." Remi pointed to the left. "Then, if you look over here" — he pointed right — "I have the spare bedroom. There is a bed in there and not much else. When you move in, you will have room for your stuff. There is another bathroom through that door." Remi pointed in front of them.

It wasn't a huge space, but it was enough for him. It might feel small with the two of them sharing it, though. And he'd have to try and not sniff his new roommate. That might cause issues.

"It's a great space."

"This is nothing. Follow me." Remi turned around and walked to his balcony. "This is why I moved in." Remi opened the door and stepped out.

He never got tired of the view. He loved baseball, and even when no one was around, he liked to look out at the field.

"When they do the big country concert, I sit out here and just listen. I'm not a big fan of that kind of music normally, but everything's better live."

"Wow. I don't know if I'd ever leave."

"Some days it's hard. I enjoy my space, for sure. It can be noisy sometimes, but I don't mind. I really like living downtown. Why don't you sit down and I'll go get us something to drink? I have lemonade, water, wine or the beer you brought."

"You know, I'd love a beer." El smiled over at him.

"Beer it is." Remington turned left the balcony.

El's smile was going to do him in. He just knew it. The more time he spent with the man, the more he had to remind himself that it was a business arrangement. But when he thought about it, there were stories of arranged marriages ending in a love match.

Nope, I really *don't need to go there.*

He grabbed them both a beer and took one of the limes out of the bag. He quartered it and put one piece in each of their beers before he headed to the balcony. When he got outside, El had his head thrown back with his eyes closed. He looked tired. He had dark circles under his eyes and there was a sad aura surrounding him.

Remi sat down to enjoy the moment of peace but El jerked in his chair.

"Sorry. Sorry."

"You look tired. Are you sure you want to do this? We can always reschedule."

"I'm good. I just nodded off for a second."

"Are you okay?"

"Yes. I really am good. And now I'm hungry for tacos."

"All right then. How about we talk about...our favorite things — or whatever else you want. That way we can get to know each other. If nothing else, I'd like to leave this situation with a friend, if you're on board."

"I could use a new friend." El winked at him.

The playful side was new. At work, El was very serious. It was nice, like he was loosening up. Remi handed him his beer. He couldn't take his eyes off El's throat as he drank. *How can drinking a beer be sexy?* To hide his interest, he took a drink from his own bottle. It hit the spot.

"Same here. So...favorite movie?"

"Diving right in, huh? Okay, I don't really have a favorite. I don't usually watch them unless it's with my mother. She loves old movies and I've seen *Gone with the Wind* more times than I am willing to admit."

"I've never seen it."

El gasped. "Then you can never meet my mother." He laughed.

"Good to know." Remi smirked.

"Now you. What's your favorite?"

"I'm a movie junkie. I love them. I don't get to the theater as much as I'd like. My dad is more of a play kind of guy. He has season tickets to the Embassy. But... Hm-m... Favorite movie... I love the funny action ones. *Hot Fuzz* or any Simon Pegg movie. If it's funny and people get shot, I'm there."

"I don't think I've heard of those."

"Which isn't acceptable. We'll have to remedy that."

Talking to El was easy. Remi didn't know why he'd expected anything different. There was an ease between the two of them, like Remi had known him for a lot longer. Granted, they worked together, but not directly, so they'd never had a real conversation.

"You'll have to make me a list," El noted.

"I will. I see a movie marathon in your future. Okay, you don't watch movies. What about reading?"

"I love to read. Sci-fi or fantasy is my favorite. I loved the Robert Jordan books, but I didn't finish the series. He died before it was done, and his wife and another author finished it out. I just didn't have the heart to see if it was a seamless passing of the baton. Stephen King and Dean Koontz are also favorites."

"I do enjoy a good Dean Koontz book. I read a lot of non-fiction too. I'm picky with my fiction."

"What is your favorite Koontz book? *Intensity* is mine," El said.

"*Odd Thomas* is mine," Remi replied.

"I loved the television adaptation. That *is* something I've watched. I was sad when the actor died."

"I haven't seen it yet because I was afraid it wouldn't live up to the books."

"It's good in its own right. You should see it."

"I'll put that on *my* to-watch list. How about *Intensity*? Wasn't there a movie made of that one? I think I did see it."

"I watched it, but the book was just so much better. They should do a remake. They do it with everything else, and that book is a classic."

"I'd watch a new movie if they made it."

"My turn to question. What's your favorite color?"

"I don't have one. Black? I don't know. What about you?" Remi laughed.

He was enjoying the back and forth. He couldn't remember the last time he'd sat down and had a conversation with someone about nothing.

"I don't have one either."

"Then why did you ask?"

El shrugged, "I don't know… It was better than 'What's your sign?'"

Remi snorted. "You've got me there."

The knock his door startled him. Remi looked down at his watch. *Shit, we've been talking for an hour.* "That must be my dad."

"Holy cow… We talked that long?"

El looked as shocked as Remi felt.

"I guess we can put my dad to work helping with the prep we never got to." Remi stood up and held out a hand to help El up.

Remi let El lead the way back inside. He wondered what dinner would bring.

Chapter Ten

El couldn't believe how easy it was to talk to Remi. They'd totally lost track of time. Remi was funny and nice, not that it should surprise him. Remi had always been a good boss.

Remi opened the door and there was Mr. Marlow. It hit him that they planned to deceive the man. El's stomach tightened with a dread he hadn't experienced before, and he didn't even know if the money would help. He might be doing this for nothing and Mr. Marlow could be hurt in the process.

The hospice nurse didn't think his mother had long, and by the time he had the money to get the experimental drug set up, she could be dead. El shook his head. *I can't think about this right now.* It would make him too sad and he needed to be upbeat, so he could be the best boyfriend ever.

After he'd greeted Remi's father, he excused himself to go into the kitchen to start on the tacos. He rummaged through the fridge and pulled out what he'd need. He should have asked Remi where all the ingredients were. He was going to need taco seasoning and there were too many cabinets to choose from.

"Hey, Remi, where's the seasoning again?" he yelled from the kitchen.

"The cabinet above the stove."

Remi sounded closer to the kitchen so he turned and saw that Remi and his dad had settled at the counter—the one he'd stood at when he'd first come in. The odd thing was how comfortable he felt in the space. He should be freaked out, but he wasn't.

"Thanks."

"I can help. Dad, you want a beer? Elros brought over some Coronas."

"Sounds good," his dad replied.

Remi walked to the fridge to grab a bottle. "The pans are to the right of the stove," he whispered to El.

They hadn't had a chance to go over where things were in the kitchen. The plan had been to start this *before* the senior Marlow got there, not to sit outside and talk for an hour.

El put all the ingredients on the counter then started to cut up some tomatoes and onions. He was going to cook those with the meat then add the beans. That way it was one big mix to put into the taco shells. There was also sour cream, salsa, jalapenos and cheese off to the side. Remi had gotten the already-shredded stuff. That was the best in his opinion. It saved a lot of time, even if it was a tad more expensive.

"I can help you guys," Mr. Marlow spoke up.

El was so in his head that he jumped a little. He hoped the other two hadn't seen it.

"Why don't you keep us company? Pull up a bar stool."

He must have missed the stools when he'd gotten there. Of course, he had been too busy looking at Remi to pay too much attention. That seemed to be his default lately.

"Mr. Marlow, it's good to see you," El said.

"Call me Jackson."

"Okay, Jackson. How has your day been?" he asked.

"Not too bad. I played some golf this morning. It was a bit chilly, but other than that, I had a good game and worked up an appetite." Jackson rubbed his belly.

"That's a good thing, because we have enough food for an army. Remi, could you start the beef?"

"Sure thing." Remi nodded.

They worked well together. It was nice and El relaxed into cooking. Remi started the meat and El put the onions and tomatoes into the mix. He'd let those simmer together for a bit before adding the beans. Remi handed him a towel to wipe his hands.

"Thanks. We can let that cook for a bit, then we can set up a taco station to put them together how we like. Sound good? The nice thing about tacos is it doesn't take too long. We'll be eating in no time." El stirred the meat before putting a lid on the pan.

"We can sit in the dining room while we wait," Remi suggested.

"Why don't you and your dad go ahead. I'm going to set stuff up here so we're ready, once the meat and beans are cooked." El smiled at them both.

"Only if you're sure. I don't mind helping." Remi squeezed his shoulder.

"I know, but go chat with your dad. I'll do this." El leaned in and brushed Remi's cheek with a kiss.

It seemed like the natural thing to do. *We're boyfriends, after all. Right?* So what if Remi looked stunned at the action, so what if it was fake. It felt right to kiss him, and he wasn't going to feel bad about it.

"Leave the boy alone, son. Let's go sit down. He has this under control." Jackson winked at him.

He took a deep breath and watched them walk the few steps to the table. El took a few seconds to gain control of himself then got back to work.

What was that?

He might not feel bad about it, but that didn't mean he wouldn't freak out a little. There apparently was an attraction between them that went both ways. The vibe on the balcony had proven that. It didn't mean he needed to act on it. He had his hands full with his mom. Granted, it was a nice distraction, but once it wasn't there anymore, his mom would still be dying.

He needed to find the plates. El should have asked where those were too, but he could figure it out. He opened a couple doors and finally found what he was looking for. There were four plates up there, so he took down three and put them on the counter by the stove. That way they could get their meat first.

After he was finished, he lined the toppings up on the back counter to hopefully keep a steady flow. He went back to check on the meat and found that it was coming right along. There was really nothing left for him to do but wait. He went over to the counter so he could see what the guys were talking about. They were both sipping their beers.

"I'd say we can eat in about ten minutes. I just need to add the spices and let it soak in for flavor and we're ready," El said.

"I was just telling Dad about how close we are to getting the green light on the apartments."

"It's about to get busy, but I'm up for the challenge." El loved his job and couldn't wait to get started.

"Since you're here for a minute, I thought I'd tell Dad about another project I plan to get involved in — one that I've wanted to do for a while, but just haven't had the chance to follow through on. I think now is the time."

"Well, this sounds interesting, son. I'm all for projects that make you passionate."

"There is an old hotel on the west side of town that has been abandoned for a while. I've called and check into it, and it's for sale. I'm going to buy it and turn it into lower income housing. It would make great little apartments. I'll be low-cost and we'd take Section Eight, as well. We have a lot of nice rentals around town, but there are people in shelters that need just a little help and I want to do something for them."

"Wow, Remi, that's awesome." El walked around the counter and, before he could think to stop, he grabbed Remi's face between his hands and kissed him.

It was spontaneous and genuine. Jackson cleared his throat and that was all it took to end the lip smacking.

"Um — Well...yeah, I'll go check on the meat." El turned and left the room.

There had been no acting on his part in that kiss. He was proud of Remi. The man didn't have to do something so altruistic. It just showed who he truly was deep inside.

The meat was ready for the spices. He dumped the packet in and added a touch of water — not the amount on the back of the pack, because that was always too much, but just enough to get it wet so it would absorb into the meat. The apartment started to smell like tacos. His stomach grumbled. He hadn't been feeding himself well the last couple of days and his body was telling him to eat something.

El was too embarrassed to go back into the dining room for now, so he busied himself in the kitchen. There wasn't much more he could do. He saw where Remi had gotten the serving spoon for the meat and he went to grab some for the salsa and cream cheese. He was running out of things to do when Remi came into the room.

What could he say? He wasn't going to apologize. They were supposed to be boyfriends.

"It smells great." Remi leaned over the pan.

"Yeah. Hungry?"

There was a tension in the room that hadn't been there earlier. It was all because of that blasted kiss. He knew it. They were uncomfortable around each other when before it had been smooth sailing.

"Very. So is Dad."

"Good. That's...good." El looked down at his hands.

Remi moved closer. El could see his feet. What he didn't expect was for Remi to put his fingers under his chin and make him look up. Remi ran his thumb over El's lips and it was all he could do not to suck the digit into his mouth. *That* would be inappropriate with the senior Marlow just a few feet away.

"Don't be embarrassed. For one, it was a great reaction—not just for being a fake boyfriend, but in general. My dad can't stop smiling and, I have to tell you, I feel a bit guilty. Not as much as I should, because— I hope it isn't just me, but I feel something here, between us."

El couldn't have looked away if he'd wanted to. He was mesmerized by Remi's bright green eyes.

"The meat's going to burn." El couldn't handle the intensity.

He slipped out of Remi's grip and went to check on the food. It was ready to go, so he leaned over the counter and called Jackson into the kitchen.

"Boys, this smells delicious," Jackson said as he grabbed a plate.

"It was all Elros," Remi said.

"Here… I forgot to put the shells by the meat." El shouldn't be nervous, but being in the same room with Remi had him on edge in a way he hadn't been before. He'd initiated a couple of kisses now. They had been in the guise of them being boyfriends, but the kisses had felt real. Even though Remi seemed to be attracted to him, too, could he handle it falling apart when the not-yet-signed contract was over? How would his heart handle losing both his boyfriend and his mother?

It was too soon to be thinking of the end. His mom was still alive and he had three months of being the handy-dandy boyfriend. Plus, he had to move in.

Oh joy.

El didn't think his life could get any more complicated. At least he hadn't signed up to actually marry Remi. He'd like to think he wouldn't sell himself for fifteen thousand dollars, but he'd do just about anything for his mother. Well…maybe not a walk down the aisle. *Maybe.*

He moved behind Remi so he could get his plate together and did his best not to think of all the naughty things he'd like to do to the man, at least not with his father in the same room. They all filled their plates then moved into the dining room. El grabbed a couple of beers and a water for himself before sitting down to a meal he hoped wouldn't be awkward. It wouldn't hurt for it to be over so he could go home, either, but that was wishful thinking — and he had a job to do.

Chapter Eleven

Remi sat down at the table with his plate of food. The evening wasn't going exactly as he'd planned. He hadn't expected the camaraderie between him and El, for one. He'd liked the guy fine at work, but this was different. And the kiss? Not that he'd complain, but it had been unexpected. In theory, he'd known that there would have to be some PDA, but in reality, he didn't know what to do with the situation. It didn't help that it seemed he was starting to lust after his fake boyfriend and have thoughts he'd never believed he'd have—a real-life boyfriend, dating, kissing, more... The 'more' really had him interested.

"So...tell me more about this housing project. I might want to invest some as well," his dad said as he sat down beside him.

"Sure. I figured I'd pay the company to do the design work and for the construction needed. It won't make a profit, but that isn't what this is about."

"I understand, son. What do you think, El?"

"I think it's wonderful. Some people just need a small helping hand to get them out of poverty. I'm hoping it will help. Fort Wayne would be a better place for it. And if Remi hired some of the tenants in the building to do maintenance and stuff, it could help even more." El looked at Remi and it hit him right in the heart.

If he hadn't already been planning on doing this for the city and the people in it, right then and there he would have done it for El, just to get him to keep looking at him like he was — with stars in his eyes. Remi could get use to that.

"Good call, El. I'll put that in with my plans. Maybe we could have an office in the building that could aid them in finding jobs or just provide general support when needed. I'll need a manager also. That person can live there, and part of their pay can be the waived rent." Now Remi was even more excited. "You should help me with it, getting it put together. That way you can see the project the whole way through. And if you have any other ideas like that, let me know and I'll see about incorporating them." Remi smiled at El.

"You two work great together." Jackson's words intruded into Remi's intense interest in El's lips.

For a second it had been like they were the only two in the room, and Remi wanted to kiss El. He didn't want to just sit there and get kissed but actually participate this time.

They were quiet for a bit, and the only sound was the crunching of tacos. It wasn't an awkward silence like Remi had been afraid of before the night had started. It was a nice family meal, just the three of them eventually talking about the day and what would happen down the road.

"These tacos are great, Elros," Mr. Marlow said.

"I have to agree with Dad. Wonderful tacos."

"It's not gourmet but thank you." There was a shy smile on El's lips.

Remi wanted to taste that smile. There was a flutter in his chest when he looked at El. It was something he hadn't experienced in a really long time and he enjoyed it, the anticipation of something new — something…not fake.

God, what a mess. Remi was falling for the one person he shouldn't. Elros was an employee and he'd contracted him to fake it until they made it. Now he didn't want that. This was going to be a tangled web of emotion and heartache, he just knew it, but frankly, he didn't care. If it felt this good while pretending, how would it feel to actually be a part of El's life? To see that shy smile every day? To hear him laugh at something silly? To argue over sci-fi movies and books? To go to bed with someone every night and wake up not feeling the silence of his lonely apartment?

"Son."

"Sorry, Dad. Lost in thought. What?" Remi asked.

"Just wondering what else the company is looking at."

"Oh, nothing big is on the horizon. Once we get started on the apartments over the theater, we can look at the low-cost housing project and see what all we need. I had an inspector go over it. He said it would need some work, but it was sound. I'm waiting for a report on what I need to get it up to code for living before I finalize the purchase. I already have the go-ahead from the city council to have it zoned for rentals once that's done. They were on board, as was the mayor, so there isn't much to do but wait for all the paperwork to clear. I think Oscar was bidding on some projects with the hospital, as they are doing the remodeling. It should keep the shop busy for most of the year."

"Sounds great, Remi. It really does. I might not say it a lot, but I sure am proud of you."

No, his dad might not always say it, but Remi knew how his father felt.

"He is a great guy, Jackson." El nodded in agreement.

"Stop… You'll make me blush."

The three of them laughed. El had a great laugh when he let himself go.

"Enough business talk. What do you boys have planned for the rest of the weekend?" Jackson looked between him and El.

"We haven't really talked about it, Dad. We might just hang around. I know I need to go over and finalize the plans for the next picnic. Sara Jo has most of it under control, but I like to help."

"I know I enjoy them every year. It's nice to get together with everyone in a relaxing atmosphere. I think the ice cream truck you guys get each year is a big draw. The guys with kids can't stop talking about it. And I won't lie. Free ice cream is always welcome." El winked at Jackson.

Everything about El was unexpected and Remi was gobbling it up like a man who hadn't eaten in a month.

"Good to know. It's just nice to be able to thank everyone for all the hard work they do for the company. I want it to feel like a family," Remi said.

"It really does. It's a wonderful business atmosphere. The people are one of the reasons I love it.

I love the work itself as well, but it's nice to be with people who share the love of the job," El reassured him.

"Remi and I love to hear that. It means we've done our best."

"Anyone want more tacos? I'm going to head in for seconds." El got up from the table.

Jackson scooted back in his chair and followed El into the kitchen. Remi just watched the two of them and contemplated the evening. He wondered if he should bring up the contract once his dad left or if he should just ask El if he wanted to date for real. *What an odd outcome.* His dad could be an evil mastermind, because maybe he'd planned this all along—not El specifically, but for Remi to find someone and end up falling for them. Not that he was falling for El, but he was beginning to think that there could be something if they wanted to explore it.

Both men walked back into the dining room, talking and laughing. El looked relaxed for the first time since he'd been on Remi's radar for this project. He wondered what had him so tense all the time. Maybe they could talk more later, and he could find out what was going on, because it had to be more than just bills.

"Not hungry?" El had leaned over to whisper.

"I'm going in now." Remi left the table to get more tacos. He also got some bowls down for the leftovers before making up more for himself to enjoy.

His dad didn't stay much longer after they'd finished eating, and Remi didn't know if that was a good or bad thing. El was in the kitchen starting clean up. Remi closed the door behind his dad and went in to help.

"You don't have to do that. I can do it later." Remi walked over to the sink.

"I don't mind. I really don't have to do much, since you have a dishwasher."

Remi went to the stove to get the meat put away. He used the bowl he'd gotten out earlier. When that was done, he went to the sink where El was rinsing off the dishes before putting them in the dishwasher. They worked side by side until everything was put away nice and neat and the dishwasher was turned on.

"How about we head out to the balcony? Unless you have to go?"

"I can stay for a bit."

"You want something to drink?" Remi opened the fridge to pull out a water for himself.

"Water is good."

Remi tossed the one in his hand to El. He caught it easily enough before going to the balcony. It was a nice night, not too cold with the stars shining bright in the sky.

"I love coming out here in the evening. I don't do it enough anymore," Remi said.

"You should make the time. It's peaceful out here," El replied.

"Tonight, it is. On game nights, it can get a little loud, but I don't mind it. I like watching what I can see of the game from up here."

"Mm-m, nice. I don't sit outside enough anymore. There's just something about a clear sky that relaxes me. I guess I need to make more time for that as well." El looked over at Remi.

Remi couldn't see his eyes too clearly, but there was a spark there. He hadn't been imagining it. He leaned closer to El.

"It is a little cold out here, though. How about we head back in?"

"Okay." El grabbed his water and went inside to sit on the couch.

Remi could have sat in the chair, but he decided to go for it. He sat down close to El.

"I'm not sure what's happening here but—" He didn't get to finish his sentence.

El took the situation into his own hands and brushed his lips against Remi's, and Remi wrapped his arms around El to bring him close, pulling their chests together. Remi leaned back and El had to follow. They had every inch touching. To Remi's way of thinking, the only thing that could make it better would be if they were naked. El pressed him down into the couch, grinding against him.

Remi opened his mouth, letting El inside. He needed more skin. Remi ran his hands up and down El's side, searching for the bottom of his shirt.

Yes.

He pushed his hands under it, running over the warm skin underneath, but it wasn't enough. Remi slid his hands farther down El's body and squeezed his ass, bringing their cocks as close as they could get while still clothed. El's moan almost made him come right then. How long had it been since he'd had someone this close to him? *Too long.*

Something was ringing. Was that his ears? *No.* What was it?

El wiggled against him. It was killing him. It took a minute for him to realize that El was getting off him. That wasn't the plan. *Where is he going?*

"My—oh, damn—my phone. Sorry." El panted. "I have to— Hold that thought."

Remi sat up, a bit disoriented.

"This is Elros. Yes." Then a pause. "No. Are you still at the house?" Another pause then, "I'll be right there."

"El?" Remi stood.

Something was wrong but he didn't know what, not from only hearing part of the conversation. El was pale and looked panicked.

"I'm so sorry. *Really* sorry. I have to go. I— Yeah, I can't be here right now. Sorry."

El ran to the closet to grab his coat and he was out of the door before Remi could say anything.

What just happened?

Chapter Twelve

El rushed down the stairs, not even waiting for the elevator. His chest hurt. If his mom died while he was out messing around, he wouldn't be able to live with himself. He ran down the street to his car like someone was chasing him. He had to get to her.

Brett had told him his mom was having trouble breathing and wasn't responding to anything, that El should get there as soon as possible because the nurse wasn't sure she would last.

He didn't remember the drive to his house. It was a blur. El was lucky he didn't get into an accident on the way.

Brett was waiting for him at the door.

"I'm sorry I disturbed your evening. Your mother is very upset that I called you."

"She's okay?"

"I don't know about that, but she is more alert now. She's in pain. I just gave her some medicine, but she isn't asleep yet."

"Thank you. I really appreciate you calling me, no matter what she thinks. If I hadn't been here —"

"I'm happy you could come so quickly. Why don't you go see her? I'm going to head out, unless you need something. She should be okay now for the night."

"No, we should be fine."

"I'll be back tomorrow."

"Thank you." El walked Brett to the door before going to see his mom.

He leaned against the doorjamb of her bedroom, watching her. She looked so pale, lying there in bed, not moving. It wasn't much different from other days. He focused on the up and down of her chest, watching her breath. She more wheezed than breathed and that couldn't be good. The months with her that he hoped for could turn into days. There was no real answer. His mom would leave on her own time, not his. He needed to get that through his head. He didn't want her in pain, but he also didn't want to lose her, but the more he wished her to stay, the worse she seemed to get.

She stirred. "Elros?"

"Yeah, Mom. I'm here."

"Sorry."

El walked on into the room and sat down by her bed. "You have nothing to be sorry about."

"I do. You were on a date. The nurse was here. It was fine."

"It *wasn't* fine, Mom. You weren't responding."

"Maybe, but I'm fine now."

"I'm calling tomorrow to find an in-home nurse who can stay here with you longer. Hospice is good, but they can only stay for so many hours. Even though we were lucky and Brett was here tonight, I really can't leave you alone anymore. I shouldn't have ever done so in the first place. I— Mom, I love you."

"I love you too, honey, more than you can possible even know."

"So, a nurse who can stay with us... I'll get it worked out so you don't have to be alone while I'm at work. You can't talk me out of it this time."

"I know. I'm sorry to be such a burden."

El reached for his mom's hand and held it. "You could *never* be a burden, but we both have to realize that this isn't getting better. We need more help. I can't be at work and worried about you here by yourself. What if Brett or I hadn't been here tonight?"

"You're such a good boy. I know it's been rough." She gasped a little for air.

"I've lived in a house filled with love. There was nothing rough about it. You've always been there for me, telling me I could do what I wanted, believing in me. To have someone who has that much faith in me? That's better than a house full of riches."

"So. Sweet." She drifted off to sleep.

His chest hurt again. If he didn't know better, he'd say he was having a heart attack—and in a way he was. His heart was breaking because he was losing the best person he'd ever known and there was nothing he could do about it. El didn't have work the next day, so he grabbed some blankets and settled into the chair. Tonight he wasn't going to leave her side.

Brett would be by tomorrow to check in. El would ask him about the twenty-four-seven nurse. He shouldn't have waited so long, but he'd let his mom talk him out of it. She'd kept saying she was fine and he'd wanted to believe her. It was going to be a long night, but he didn't care.

Now that his mom was sleeping, he could think about what had happened earlier. It had been unexpected, to say the least. The chemistry between him and Remi was off the charts. But as much as he'd like to become more than a fake boyfriend, his mom needed his full attention right now. At least they hadn't signed any contract yet. He was going to have to tell Remi they could only be friends. It was for the best. He couldn't think of any future for himself at this point in time. For now, he had to watch his mother breathe. As long as her chest moved, he could feel safe in the knowledge that she would be around for a little longer.

As he drifted off to sleep, he thought of Remi's lips — how they'd tasted and how wonderful it had felt to be pressed up against him. It had been so long since he'd had any type of physical contact with anyone or anything other than his hand, that he'd nearly come from just a kiss. *A kiss*! It seemed impossible, and if he hadn't felt it for himself, he wouldn't have believed it. Dreams… The kiss haunted his dreams.

A naked Remi in front of him and all he wanted to do was lick his body from head to toe.

El jerked awake. He was hard. And very uncomfortable, since he was in a chair in his mom's room.

"Honey, go to bed," she said softly. "I'll be here in the morning. I promise."

He got up and leaned over to kiss her on the forehead. "I'm going to hold you to that," he rasped.

For now, he'd have to take it one day at a time. Now he was going to his room to dream more about a man he shouldn't desire.

* * * *

The weekend had come to an end sooner than El wanted. Sunday hadn't been too bad. It had been mostly him and his mom, and he'd forgotten to ask Brett about a full-time nurse when he'd stopped by. He should have called Remi. He should probably have explained why he'd rushed out Saturday night, but the day had passed too fast and he hadn't gotten around to it.

I'll talk to him today and explain.

The drive to work was quick. He went to see if Remi was in yet, but his office was empty. Sara Jo wasn't there either. For now, he'd get some coffee and work. Maybe he could talk to Remi at lunch before heading home.

He didn't want to leave his mom alone anymore. At lunch he would remember to ask Brett for a recommendation for a twenty-four-hour nurse. He'd have to talk to Remi about his mom too, because when she died—God, it was when, not if—but *when* she died, he was going to need time. No matter how much he tried to harden himself to the fact she was leaving him, he knew that when the time came, he wouldn't be worth anything. And he wasn't going to put his work and other people's safety on the line when he was unstable.

"Hey, El, how's your mom?" Sara Jo leaned on his door.

"God, it's not good. I—" He hung his head, despondent.

Sara Jo walked into his office then closed the door behind her before pulling him into a hug. El wrapped his arms around her, soaking in the comfort. He couldn't stay there too long, however, or he'd break down. He was at work and that wasn't appropriate. He didn't want to act like a baby where others could see him.

"She doesn't have long, Sara Jo. She stopped breathing for a bit last night. I was over at Remi's. His dad had left and we were on the couch when my phone rang. I was kissing him and — I had to run out. I have no idea what he thinks of me."

"Wait! Hold on a minute. You *what*? You were *where*? You were with *who*? And doing *what*?"

"Oh, shit. I forgot to tell you! So much has happened."

"You and *Remi*?" Sara Jo gasped out.

"It's all fake."

"Start from the beginning," she demanded.

"So…remember when you got me an appointment with him?"

"Yes."

"I was asking for overtime, but I already had too many hours in, so he asked me to be his boyfriend," El explained.

"*What!*"

"Not for real. I guess his dad is on him to find someone, so he wanted me to pretend to be his boyfriend for a few months. We'll see how it goes. On Saturday I made tacos for Remi and his dad. It was nice."

"And the kissing?" Now Sara Jo was grinning.

"That just…kinda happened. But he must think something's wrong with me because of how fast I left. But, it wasn't him. The hospice nurse called me. He was there for about an hour."

"Oh no, you had to call in hospice?"

"I did. I'm going to have to get a full-time nurse too. She shouldn't be by herself. I am such a failure. What if something happens when someone isn't there? What if I walk in after work and she's gone because she fell and no one was there to help her?"

"You are the best son in the world. You love your mom more than anything." Sara Jo patted his shoulder.

"I know. Everything is so confusing. And now, this fake thing with Remi makes my heart ache. When we kissed, it was so real. What if it was just practice or I'm seeing something that isn't there?" El put his head in his hands.

"Honey, he shouldn't have taken advantage of you like that."

"He didn't. He has no idea about my mom. I haven't said anything to anyone here at work."

"You need to talk to someone, El. Your whole world is crashing down around you and it can't be good for you."

"I'm talking to you, aren't I?"

"You know what I mean, El."

"I do. Thank you for checking on me."

"You just keep me in the loop, you understand? And I want more details about you and Remi, but I have to go to work."

"Don't interrogate him!"

"Who? Me?"

"Yes, you. He knows I was going to tell you. It was something we agreed on when we talked about it. So you can say something, but that's it." El pointed a finger at Sara Jo.

"Fine. But I will be having a talk with him. He can't hurt you...not on my watch." Sara Jo gave him one more hug before leaving the office.

El was happy she'd shown up. He didn't know how bad he'd needed to talk to someone. It was time to tell Remi what was going on. It would help explain what had happened on Saturday.

Work went by fast after his visit from Sara Jo. It was lunch before he knew it. He was going to see if Remi was in and get this talk out of the way before heading home. He really needed to talk to Brett to see who he would recommend, then find out if the insurance would take care of it. Hell, even if it didn't, they could bill him. They needed that nurse.

He walked up to Remi's office. Sara Jo was at her desk.

"Is he in?"

"Yeah, hold on a second and I'll buzz him."

Chapter Thirteen

Remi couldn't believe he was still upset over the weekend. It had started out so good, but then El had up and left him with no real explanation. Remi knew he shouldn't have followed El home, but he was worried about him.

It was on him that he'd seen some guy walk out of El's house. What had he been doing there? El had told him he didn't have a boyfriend, but why would some guy be walking out of the house so late?

And why was he taking that to heart? He had no real claim on El. Hell, they'd never signed the contract and they weren't dating for real. He had no right to be as upset as he was, but he'd thought they had something going on between them. El had felt it too. He had to...

Or is that wishful thinking on my part? It was so confusing. Plus, he hadn't heard from El the rest of the weekend. The more he thought about it, the more pissed off he got. Work had sucked today. He couldn't concentrate and thankfully he hadn't seen El. If he had, he was afraid he'd have said something that he shouldn't. They still had to work together, and he had promised that the fake boyfriend thing wouldn't interfere with the job.

He was a grown-up. He needed to put his feelings for El in a box. He was untouchable. They would fake it in front of his dad and that would be it.

Remi thought about how El had felt on top of him, how his lips had been so soft. They could build from that, but not if El was lying about having a boyfriend.

God, he was back to thinking he had a claim on an employee. It was getting him nowhere. Later today, he had an appointment out at the Embassy where they were renovating the hotel above the theater into luxury apartments. It would do him good to get out of the building and immerse himself the job.

"Mr. Marlow, Elros is here to see you."

Fuck. He needed to put his big boy pants on. He could do this.

He pressed the intercom button. "Send him in."

Remi went to his chair behind his desk, giving him the position of power. He was going to need it for this confrontation.

Stop. It isn't a confrontation. He owes you nothing.

When the door opened, he didn't expect to feel hurt, but he was.

"Hi, Remi." El shut the door behind him, but it didn't latch.

"El." Remi gave him a nod.

El sat down in the chair in front of the desk. He was fidgeting with his shirt. It was like a replay of the first meeting. It was endearing, but he had to harden his heart. This wasn't going anywhere. He had to remember that.

"I wanted to apologize."

"No need."

"I had a great time on Saturday and I really like your dad."

"Dinner was wonderful." He hated this cold façade he was putting on, but he needed to take care of himself. That was the way it had always been. No matter what his dad thought, he was better off alone. He'd seen what it had done to his dad when his mom had died. Now Remi wouldn't have to worry about that happening to him.

Elros looked at him curiously then his face dropped and he said, "Thank you. Yeah, sorry to interrupt your day. I need to head home. I'll be back after lunch." His shoulders slumped, and he looked sad.

Remi nodded and watched him walk off. There was some mumbling outside his office. He couldn't catch what was said, but it wasn't happy.

Remi let out a sigh. This was what happened when he had stupid ideas that involved other people. He should stick to buildings. They couldn't hurt him.

He turned on the computer so he could go through his emails before he went out to lunch. He was going to meet the owners of the theater project for a meal before they went on a walk-through. He wanted to take some measurements and pictures.

His door slammed. "What was *that*?"

He jumped. Sara Jo stood in front of him with her hands on her hips.

"Excuse me?"

"El just left here, and it isn't bad enough he started the day sad, but he just looked like a puppy that had been kicked. What did you say to him?"

"That...dinner was good?"

"That can't be it."

"Look… I know you're friends, but this is between us."

"Oh, really? He told me about this deal you put on the table. Don't you think that's taking advantage of him while he's down?"

"He knew what he was getting into. I didn't do anything to him. He's the one with a boyfriend," he shouted. It was a good thing Sara Jo had had the hindsight to shut the door.

"What are you even talking about?" Sara Jo crossed her arms.

"I saw the guy coming out of his house on Saturday night."

"Yeah, you have no idea what you're talking about. There is no guy."

"I saw him with my own two eyes."

"You're mistaken, and maybe instead of pulling this passive-aggressive bullshit, you should—I don't know—talk to him?" She threw her hands up in the air.

"So, who was the guy?"

"I am not the middleman here. You need to talk to him—and not be so cold. I like you, Mr. Marlow. You're a great boss. You really are, and I don't like overstepping, but El is hurting right now, and he could use at least a friend, more than just me. So, talk to him." She pointed a finger at him, turned and walked out of the office.

That was unexpected. There was so much happening that he had no control over. What had she meant, that he didn't know what he was talking about? There had been a guy. He'd seen him. El had been sad and in a panic. Why would the guy have left if he was a boyfriend? Wouldn't he have stayed to comfort El? Remi put his head in his hands.

* * * *

Remi pulled up to the office. He'd had a nice walk-through of the theater project. He was a little concerned that the company was throwing out old claw-foot tubs and sinks that were original to the previous hotel accommodations from the building. There had to be someone he could talk to about getting rid of that kind of stuff, maybe call in a salvage company. People would pay for those tubs. They'd just been sitting in the old hotel rooms for years. There was really nothing wrong with them that a little cleaning up couldn't fix. It would be upsetting if they just went to the landfill.

The company that owned the property wanted it done fast. They were on target for now. He'd done some measurements of the handrail, had taken some pictures for the detailers. He loved that part of the job, getting a feel for the place and thinking about how it would look when it was finished.

El's car was parked in his spot. Remi should be an adult and talk to him, tell him what he'd seen and find out what had been going on. He didn't want to be one of those guys who misunderstood something because he didn't communicate. He hated it when that happened in books or in movies. With a heavy sigh, he left the car and headed in. When he got to his office, Sara Jo gave him the cold shoulder. He didn't like it when she was upset, and it seemed somehow like this was his fault.

He put his keys in his desk drawer, along with his phone. At least lunch had been nice. They had eaten at a local café close to the theater. He wondered if El would like it. *And there it is...* He was still thinking about El. It was time to go talk to him. He walked over to El's office and knocked on the door.

"Yes." El didn't even look up.

"I was just checking on you," Remi said.

This time he did look up. His eyes were red, like he'd been crying.

"I'm good," Elros replied.

Remi walked in and shut the door behind him. "I don't think so. You rushed out of my place and I followed you home."

"You did *what* now?"

"I was worried, El. You left so fast and I didn't know if you'd get home safe."

"Why didn't you come in?"

"There was a guy walking out and —"

El gave a tired laugh. "No wonder you were acting weird." He shook his head.

"You really don't owe me anything," Remi said.

"No, I don't, but I'll tell you anyway. I should have told you a while ago and I wouldn't have been so stressed. That was Brett, the hospice nurse. My mom is dying. It's why I have been going home at lunch. She has been there by herself. When you propositioned me, she told me to go through with it because she wanted me to live my life. So, I said yes. I've been a horrible son, leaving her alone when she is so sick and in pain, but she keeps telling me she's fine. Until you asked me to be your boyfriend... It was then she requested the nurse. Now I need to get someone full time. She wasn't breathing. That was the call I got."

"Oh, Elros. You should have said something, even before you came to my office. We could have done something."

"No, you really couldn't have. The only thing that would have helped was money, so I could get her into a trial with some experimental drugs that insurance won't pay for."

"That's why you needed the overtime..." Remi moved closer to El's desk.

"Yes."

"I can give you the money now. Screw the contract. Just—"

"Thanks, Remi. I really appreciate that, but it won't help. It's too late. It could be days or weeks, but not much longer. That's why I'm getting the nurse. I hired someone during lunchtime who was recommended by the hospice nurse. Mom can't be by herself anymore, no matter how much she might want to be."

"I am *so* sorry. I was being an ass. I should have talked to you. I knew something was wrong, but all I could think about was some guy coming out of your place and I freaked."

"You did?" El smiled.

"You don't have to be so happy about it."

"You know we aren't real boyfriends, right?" Now El smirked at him.

"About that." Remi sat on the edge of El's desk. "We never got around to signing the contract."

"No, we didn't."

"So, who's to say we can't... I don't know...date?" Remi asked.

"Remi, are you asking me out?"

"Yes."

"I thought you didn't date."

"I didn't think I did, until I met you," he replied honestly.

"I've worked at this company for twelve years."

"True, but I didn't consider you boyfriend material."

"Gee, thanks, Remi."

"Now, don't be that way. You know what I mean. You work for me. Not directly, but your boss reports to me. I own the company and work isn't a dating pool for me," he explained again.

"Thank you for coming to talk to me."

"I'm serious about dating, El. If it doesn't stick, we can be friends. I'm not going to jeopardize your job."

"No, but you'll give me the cold shoulder," El said.

"Yes, *but* I did come talk to you instead of letting it stew."

"Sara Jo yelled at you, didn't she?"

Remi scratched the back of his neck. "Maybe."

El threw his head back and laughed. It was much better than seeing him so sad, though it was going to get worse before it got better. Remi had been younger when his mother had died, but the hurt had never gone away. He vowed right then and there to help El get through this in any way he could.

"Why don't you come to dinner? I'd like you to meet my mom," Elros said.

"Are you sure about that?"

"Yes. If we're going to date and not fake it, I want— I'd like you to meet her before she dies. That sounds bad, but— God, I'm going to miss her, and if we're going to be together, she should meet you too. I think it will make her feel better about leaving me. I love her and she's in pain."

"Come here." Remi stood and gathered El close for a hug.

Everyone needed a hug and he'd be the strong one for El, to hold him when things got bad. He closed his eyes and thanked God for another chance. He was going to get Sara Jo a big box of chocolates and remember not to be so stupid next time. Talking was always better than speculating.

"Dinner it is. I'd love to meet your mom. Fair is fair. But…do I have to cook?"

El laughed again.

It was a beautiful sound.

Chapter Fourteen

El couldn't believe that he'd invited Remi over for dinner. Spontaneous invitations seemed to be his thing now. Remi had been jealous. El hadn't seen that coming. The cold shoulder from Remi that morning hadn't felt good, and he worried that if they didn't keep dating, it would happen again. But like his mother always said, *'We only live once'*. He'd spent a lot of the last few years taking care of his mom — not that he'd trade anything for his time with her — but maybe he could have a little time for himself, even if only for a little while.

Remi followed him to his house, like he'd done before. Of course, El'd had no idea on Saturday that Remi had done it because he'd been too focused on getting home and hoping his mom wasn't dead. He had no idea what shape she'd be in tonight, but he needed Remi to meet the most important person in his life. The nurse, Susie, who Brett had recommended and the person he'd spoken with during lunchtime after he'd cleared it with insurance, should be there. He'd asked Brett to set her up in the spare room when she arrived.

El pulled up to the house and parked. He waited until Remi got out of his car before heading to the house.

"I'm not sure how Mom's going to be. I just got it set up during lunch for her to have a nurse all day and night. Brett called me a bit ago to tell me the new nurse had arrived and he was setting her up in the spare bedroom before he left."

"I don't have to stay for long," Remi assured him.

"We'll play it by ear." El let himself into the house.

The new round-the-clock nurse was in the living room, reading a book. When they entered the room, she stood.

"Hello, Mr. Carter. It's nice to meet you in person. Your mother has been sleeping on and off for the past hour. Nothing has changed since I arrived and, from what Brett told me, since lunch."

"Please, it's Elros. This is Remington. Remi, this is Susie." He turned back to her. "Sit down. I'm just going to fix some dinner. Would you like some?"

"That would be nice. Thank you."

"Don't thank me yet. I'm just going to check on Mom for a minute and I'll be right out. Remi, you can have a seat. We can start cooking after I'm done."

"We?" Remi looked at him wide-eyed.

"That was the royal 'we', meaning me." El laughed.

He walked into the room and sadness washed over him. His mother looked so small lying in her bed. El walked closer and brushed his fingers across her forehead.

"El?" she asked.

"Yeah, Mom, it's me."

"Happy...you're home."

"I brought company, if you feel up to meeting someone," El said.

"Who? Could I have...some water?"

"Sure thing." There was a carafe on the bedside table.

He poured her a small glass then put his hand under her head to lift her a tad, to make it easier for her to drink.

"Thanks."

"As to your question, I brought home my boss."

"Your fake boyfriend?" his mother asked.

"Well...maybe not anymore."

"What?" She smiled. He hadn't seen that in a while.

"Yep. Guess he saw Brett leaving the house and got jealous. We talked today and decided to try for real." El shrugged.

"How. Wonderful. Yes... I want to meet him."

"I'm going to fix dinner. You hungry?"

"I could try some broth. Maybe." She patted his hand.

"Okay, you rest, Mom. I'll come get you when it's ready."

El left the room. He shut the door behind him and leaned against it. Then he took a deep breath, clutched his chest and bent over. It was hard to see her looking so fragile. They had gone from 'We should talk about this' to 'It's happening *now*'.

Once he got himself together, he went back to the living room.

"Mom will come out once we have dinner ready. She's going to try some broth."

"That's great. She needs to have something. Is broth the only thing she's been keeping down?" Susie asked.

"Yes. I wish she would eat more, but she just throws it up. I'm going to head into the kitchen.

Remi followed him. "I'm sorry." He moved behind El and wrapped his arms around him.

El leaned back against him, soaking in the comfort. "Thanks, Remi."

"I'm here if you need me. Anytime, day or night. Okay?"

All El could do was nod. He gave himself a minute to enjoy the warmth of Remi's body before he made himself move.

"We don't have a lot. I guess I should have thought about that before I invited you over. I have some broth to warm up for mom. Let me look through the pantry and see what I can find." Elros walked into the kitchen and looked around. "Let me see... We have rice, soup... Oh! I know... How does pasta sound? I've got some noodles and sauce. Let me check the freezer — Yep, I have garlic bread too."

"That sounds wonderful, and it's actually something I could help with," Remi said.

"Great. Let me grab a pot and I'll have you get the water ready. I know I have a few things to doctor up the sauce." El grabbed what he needed and handed off the pot to Remi, so he could get the water started. "The salt is on the stove and I'll grab some oil for you."

"Salt? Oil?"

"Yes, to put in the water."

"I guess you learn something new every day. I just boil water. How much of each?" Remi asked when El handed him the oil.

"Just shake the salt in there for a second then add a dash of oil. The salt is for flavor and the oil makes it so the noodles don't stick together."

They worked in silence for a few minutes. The water was soon on the stove, so El got a small pan out and started to heat up the sauce. He'd let it simmer for a bit while the noodles cooked.

"This is nice," Remi said.

El looked over at his boss and potential real boyfriend, who was leaning against the counter.

"What?"

"Cooking with you. I mean, tacos were nice, but this feels like I'm actually helping."

"You are." El laughed. "Why don't you keep helping and grab the garlic bread out of the freezer. Let me know what I need to set the oven at, so we can get it preheated."

"Wow, you preheat too?" Remi gave him a look of faked awe.

"You rebel, you. I bet you put stuff in the oven before you even turn it on," El retorted.

"I plead the fifth." Remi looked at the package he'd pulled from the freezer. "It says three-fifty."

God, I needed this. Spending time with Remi helped him in ways El hadn't realized that he needed. "That means you're guilty," El accused. He moved to turn the oven on.

"And what would I be charged with?"

"Crimes against cooking."

"That's not a real thing." Remi snorted.

"Well, you asked." El shrugged.

"I guess I did." Remi put the bread in the oven while El watched him.

El shook his head. The oven hadn't really had time to get up to temperature, but he was going to let that slide.

Remi really was an attractive guy. And El was learning that it wasn't just Remi's outer appearance. He was a great person as well. If things worked out, El would be a lucky man.

"You two…are…having…fun."

El turned to see his mom struggling through the doorway. He hurried toward her and helped her to a chair.

"Mom, you should have waited until I could come get you."

She waved him off. "It's…good to get…up. And Susie was watching me."

El didn't like the way she was breathing. He looked over to see the nurse walking in. He closed his eyes for a second to get himself under control. *Maybe this isn't such a good idea.*

Chapter Fifteen

Remi lost his joy when El's mom walked into the room. She looked really bad, and he could see why El was so worried. *God, I wish El had come to me sooner.* Remi would have gotten her into that experimental trial.

El looked heartbroken. He wanted to hug him close and never let him go. This was such a horrible situation. El closed his eyes and Remi moved closer to clutch his shoulder.

"Mom, this is Remington Marlow. Remi, this is my mom, Kathleen."

"Ma'am." He held out his hand.

"None of that. Call me…Kathleen."

"Kathleen it is." He leaned over and kissed her hand.

"Oh, you!" She smiled at him. It brightened up her face.

He could see a little of El in her features. They had the same brown eyes, and he would guess she'd been a brunette in her time.

"Your son is showing me how to make pasta the correct way."

"He'd know. That's something he's been making for a really long time. His sauce is much better than anything I've ever been able to come up with."

"Well, the water is boiling, so I'm going to add the noodles. I think El's going to work on the sauce. Why don't you two beautiful ladies sit and watch us?" Remi winked.

He moved to the stove and waited for El to join him.

"I'm sorry, El."

"Yeah. Thanks, Remi. It sucks." El took a deep breath. "But, we're living a day at a time now. It's just the way it has to be."

"Remember that I'm here for you." Remi bumped his shoulder against El's.

They worked in silence for a few minutes. Remi watched El toss things into the sauce. There were fresh tomatoes, a few green things, some garlic, salt and pepper. He couldn't wait to taste it. Remi tossed the penne pasta into the boiling water and checked on the bread. It looked like things might come together around the same time.

"Remi, you can go sit with Susie and Mom," El said. "I'll finish up. Everything's almost done."

"I can get plates and stuff out. Just direct me where to find things."

El nodded toward the cabinet to the left of him. "The plates are up there. Under them in the drawer is the silverware."

Remi busied himself with getting out what they would need to eat. He set it all on the counter next to the stove. He didn't go to the table. Instead, he watched El finish off the pasta. He threw it into the sauce and tossed. Usually he'd just added the sauce to his serving, he'd never added everything together.

"Why don't you get you and Susie some food?" El asked. "I'm going to warm up some broth for Mom."

Remi nodded and put some pasta on two plates. He added a piece of garlic bread before going to the table. He put one in front of Susie and one by an empty chair, but he didn't sit. He went to put another plate together. By that time, El had the broth warmed.

El moved to the table and gave it to his mom.

"It's nice to meet you." Kathleen smiled at him, but she didn't eat.

"I'm happy El let me come for dinner tonight."

"You're going" — she took a breath and it rattled a bit — "to treat him…right."

"Yes, ma'am, that is the plan."

"None of this fake…crap," she said with effort.

"No. It's all real," Remi assured her.

"Mom!" El interrupted.

"Don't…Mom…me." She wagged a finger at him.

It was hard for Remi to watch the interplay between mother and son. It was so obvious how sick she was. She was having such trouble breathing and talking at the same time. She wasn't eating. He could tell she was humoring El by accepting the broth.

"This is really good, guys," Susie piped up, but she watched Kathleen all the while.

The nurse looked worried too. He didn't realize how happy he should be that his own mom had died quickly and hadn't had this lingering illness.

"Thanks, Susie. Mom, how about I take you back to your room." El stood.

"I think…that's best. Thank you…for meeting… me… Remi."

Remi stood and helped Kathleen out of her chair. "The honor was mine." He kissed her cheek before going back to his seat.

He watched El walk his mom out of the kitchen then said, "It's not good, is it, Susie?"

"I can't really discuss it with you…"

"It's okay. I think I have my answer."

They continued to eat in silence for a few minutes before El returned.

"Susie, she's settled for the night. She fell asleep almost as soon as her head hit the pillow, but not without telling me to go home with Remi." El laughed.

There was no joy in his tone. The sadness laced through it broke Remi's heart.

"Don't worry about us here. You go on and head out for the night." Susie took her plate to the sink, rinsed it off, put it in the dishwasher and left the kitchen.

"You don't have to go home with me. I mean, though, I wouldn't say no," Remi said.

"I'm trying to live every day, and that's what she wants, so, I'm going to go with you, if that's okay?" El looked at him with a shy smile.

"I would love it if you came home with me and stayed. We can sit on the balcony for a bit and look at the stars, maybe get a little drunk. I'm up for anything. And—I won't lie—I'd like you to stay over, even if it's only so I can hold you through the night. I'm hurting for you, El. I can't imagine what you're feeling."

"You've lost your mom," El stated.

"Yes, but it was so fast. Her car crashed, and it was over. How long has this been going on?"

"God… Years? She was in remission for a while."

"You should have come to me sooner. If I had known you needed money for her, I would have given it to you. I had no idea she was this bad." Remi got up so he could hug El. He needed to touch him, to help him grieve.

"I didn't want to put my life out there. Work was work. Don't get me wrong, the company is wonderful, but I wanted to handle this. Then the cancer came back, and it wasn't going away. She couldn't do chemo anymore. I don't understand everything, but it has to do with her blood, I guess, and her body not being able to handle it. I just know that she hurts, and I can't do anything. She has *always* been there for me, pushing me to be everything I wanted."

Remi wrapped his arms around El and gave him a squeeze.

Chapter Sixteen

El took what comfort he could from Remi. It wasn't going to get any better. He knew that, but God, Remi's arms felt wonderful. Did he want to leave his mom, when she could slip away at any moment? *No.* But he'd promised her he'd live his life to his fullest. She was sleeping for now, Susie would watch over her and hopefully she still would be sleeping peacefully when he got back.

He didn't plan to spend the night or anything, just take a little time to breathe. This was the calm before the storm.

"Let me finish cleaning up and we can go." El reluctantly left the warmth Remi offered.

"I'll help. We'll get done faster. And, you don't have to come over." Remi rubbed his hands up and down El's arms. It was comforting, and he needed as much of that as he could get.

"I promised her. It's what she wants. She's happy we're going to give it a go—real dating and all. She's worried about leaving me alone."

"It's just the two of you?"

El shrugged. "Yeah, I don't know my dad. He left when I was little. I have Sara Jo, so I told Mom I'd be okay." El moved to the sink and clutched the edge, gripping it so tight that his knuckles turned white. "I'm not going to be okay." El covered his mouth with his hand to stifle the sob.

"Oh, El… I wish I could do something for you."

"You are. Just you being here helps. I don't know what I would have done if you hadn't been with me tonight."

"Okay, let's get this kitchen clean. Why don't I rinse and put everything in the dishwasher? How about you go check on your mom again before we leave?"

El brushed his lips against Remi's cheek and left him in the kitchen. Remi was so understanding. He'd guessed that El wouldn't want to leave before he saw his mom one more time. He went to his mom's room. She was asleep, so he wasn't going to disturb her. He looked down at her and listened to her breathing. *I shouldn't leave.*

He closed his eyes and stood for a moment, not moving, just being in the same room with her in a way he might not be able to for long. It was hard—waiting for her to pass. On one hand, it would be better for her, but it was going to hurt like a bitch for him. Sure, everyone died, but he thought he'd have more time with her. He was sure everyone felt that way when they lost a parent.

Remi was in the living room waiting for him when he returned.

"You all ready?"

"Yeah, she's still sleeping for now. Susie, do you need anything before I leave? Are you sure it's okay for me to go?"

"No, we're good here. I have your number if anything changes. You've been at this for months. You need to take care of you as well. Okay? Don't worry about us."

"I know. She's already told me if she goes, she goes, but—"

"Why don't you follow me to my place, El? That way, if you need to hurry back, you don't have to worry about me getting you here. Will that make you feel better?"

El didn't think anything was going to make him feel better at this point, but he'd take the little bits that he could.

"Sounds great. Susie, don't hesitate to call." El picked up his keys from an end table by the door. "I'm ready." El nodded to Susie and they left.

"I'm serious, El. You don't have to come to my place," Remi offered as they walked out.

"I think I need to, just a few hours to clear my head. And work tomorrow will help too."

"Maybe you should take some family leave," Remi suggested.

They walked down the steps together, side by side. Remi grabbed his hand and held it tight.

"I will. I should have taken it a month ago. My mom is very stubborn, and she didn't want me to worry, so I didn't take any. I want to finish out this week, then I'll fill out any paperwork I need to."

"She seems like a great lady."

El swallowed hard, "Yeah, the best mom ever. Okay"—he clapped his hands together—"I'll follow you to your place." El palmed Remi's cheek and ran his thumb over his plump lips.

El hadn't known how much he needed someone other than Sara Jo in his life. Between Sara Jo and Remi, they might be able to help him get through the next few weeks, if he was lucky.

He got behind the wheel of his car and waited for Remi to drive past. God, he really didn't want his mom to hurt anymore, but he did want to honor her wishes to die at home. He'd worry about the rest later. This was about her, not him.

The radio was playing a sad song. There was no way he could listen to something like that. He turned the station and blasted a pop song he knew the words to and sang as loud as he could with the windows rolled down. The air was chilly, but wonderful on his face.

It was about twenty minutes to Remi's place. He got through a few songs. His voice was raw from all the singing, but he was in a better mood. He would do his best to push his mom from his thoughts, at least for the next couple of hours, and try not to feel guilty about it. He parked the car in the parking garage and waited for Remi to park in his assigned space so they could walk to his place together. Maybe they'd hold hands again. That had been nice. But El wanted so much more than just hands. *Full body contact would be even better.*

"How about a drink?" Remi said after he opened his door.

"God, yes." It might not be the best idea, but it could help him chill out some.

"You've got it. Beer?"

"Whiskey?" El countered.

"Whiskey it is."

"Just one shot, then a beer would be nice. I have to drive home, so I want to pace myself." El rubbed his palms on his pants.

He waited for Remi to walk into the kitchen before he sat on the couch. Remi's place was just as comforting as it had been the first time. For a rental unit, it was kind of quiet. Of course, there was no game or any other event going on tonight. It would be nice to live here when the farmer's market was going on—just a walk to the ball field and back home... It would be like having a grocery store in his back yard.

"Here." Remi handed him a shot.

El threw it back. "Good," he rasped out. It was firey going down.

Remi held out his hand for the shot glass and switched it with a beer. El's stomach burned from the whiskey. It hadn't been a great idea, but tonight wasn't for good ideas. It was for living in the moment. And right now, that moment was drinking.

He sipped the beer. It was a local IPA. *Not too bad.* El didn't drink a lot, but beer was one of his guilty pleasures. One day he might try his hand at making his own. He'd need a hobby.

"Do you want to talk about it?" Remi settled in next to him.

Their thighs touched. Remi was so close.

"Not yet. Maybe never. I don't know." El shrugged and took another sip of beer.

"It's rough. I don't know if I was lucky or not, but my mom didn't suffer. I lost her and there is still a hole in my heart from missing her, but she didn't suffer."

"Yeah."

"Sorry... We aren't talking about this. What would you like to talk about?"

El put his beer on the coffee table. "I don't want to talk." He leaned in closer, so he could brush his lips against Remi's.

That was what he wanted, what he needed — to feel something good. He was empty yet filled with grief. He wanted time to stop, to be in this moment, in Remi's arms forever. Remi gathered him close, pulling El on top of him. They were back to the position they had been in the night he'd had to run out to check on — *No, I'm not going there*. God, it was wonderful being held tight. He forgot how much he loved kissing. Just a taste of Remi had him craving more.

"I don't know if—" Remi whispered against El's lips.

"Don't think, Remi, just feel. I need this. I need *you*."

"But we just went from fake boyfriends to dating. Don't you think this might be too fast?"

"Shh. It isn't too fast. We've been skirting this since I agreed to move in with you."

"We should probably hold off on that."

El chuckled. "You think?" He nuzzled Remi's neck.

"Now, now… Don't laugh at me or I won't put out."

El moved his hand between them to squeeze Remi's dick. "I don't think you'll deny me."

Remi moaned. The sound went right to El's cock. He wanted to suck Remi off, to taste him. Nothing was going to stop him from his goal.

He moved off the couch and sat on his haunches between Remi's legs.

"I'm going to taste you. I need to." El unbuttoned Remi's pants and eased the zipper down. "Lift up." El pulled Remi's pants and briefs down to his ankles before he realized he'd forgotten his shoes. He made quick work of them.

"El—"

"Just relax." El ran a finger down Remi's thigh. All that glorious skin was right in front of him.

"I should be—" Remi sucked in a breath.

Yeah, he had Remi where he wanted him, at his mercy. El pulled Remi's pants and underwear the rest of the way off and threw them to the side. *God, he's beautiful. Every hard inch of him.* Remi leaned forward so he could take his shirt off. He was naked on the couch and El enjoyed the view. Remi didn't have much chest hair, but he had a dark blond trail leading to his hard dick. El licked his lips, inched closer and licked the head before sucking it into his mouth. He stayed there, swirling his tongue under the tip.

"Mm-m." He hummed, the vibration tingling his lips.

His pants were becoming uncomfortable with his cock straining against the zipper. But the pain kept him on edge.

"God, you're good at this." Remi carded his hands through El's hair. He tugged it, not too hard, but enough that El felt it down to his toes.

El moved to his knees so he'd have a better position to take Remi all the way in. He moved back up and squeezed Remi's thighs.

"Fuck." Remi moved his hips, thrusting, pushing deeper and deeper. "We need to take this to the bedroom and get you out of those clothes."

El pulled off Remi's dick. "If you can think and talk, I'm doing something wrong." El wiped a hand across his mouth.

"Untrue. I just want to reciprocate, and it will be easier if we're lying down." Remi winked at him.

El got up off the floor and held a hand out to Remi. He pulled him off the couch. "Lead the way."

It had been a while since he'd felt this good. As a matter of fact, he couldn't remember the last time he'd tingled all over and wanted to have someone balls-deep inside him. The attraction between him and Remi had built over the week. He was thankful for the day he'd walked into that office and asked for overtime.

Remi turned to wrap his arms around El, bringing him in for a kiss.

Chapter Seventeen

El felt wonderful in his arms. Their bodies fit together like they had been made that way. And boy, did El have a mouth on him. He would have come right there in the living room, but Remi wanted to taste El so bad that it hurt.

Remi turned on the bedroom light because he wanted to see what he was doing.

"You're overdressed." Remi tugged El's shirt over his chest.

"You're right." El unbuckled his pants and kicked off his shoes before wiggling out of his jeans.

He could stand there all night looking at El, but he needed more. Remi took El's hand and tugged him to the bed. It was time they got horizontal. He wanted El to forget, just for a little while.

"El, God, you're beautiful."

"Mm-m… Not as gorgeous as you. I could look at you all day, but right now I'm going to do more than look, Remi. I plan on a lot more touching."

To prove his point, El ran a finger down Remi's chest. Remi rose up onto his elbows to watch. It was erotic in an unexpected way. He bit his bottom lip, so he wouldn't moan.

"Remi, I want your sounds," El said.

"You're bossy."

"I just know what I like. The noises you make turn me on. I'm so hard right now."

"I see that. Why don't I take care of that for you?" Remi sat up so he could crawl to the end of the bed. He slid onto his stomach and kissed El's thigh.

"Move over on top of me so I can finish what I started in the living room."

Remi wasn't a fool. He moved, taking some of his weight on his elbows so he didn't crush El.

"Mm-m... Your lips are heaven on my cock," Remi said.

El hummed. It was going to be his undoing for sure. No way was he going to come before El did. Remi sucked on the tip of El's dick. He must have liked what Remi did because he was groaning around Remi's cock, causing the sensation to go right to his balls. It was going to be over before it had even really started. No way did he want that. He bobbed up and down, sucking hard on every inch of El's shaft. He stuck his tongue out, licking as he sucked.

"Remi. Too... Oh, my fucking God. Too fast. I'm gonna come. Gah!"

It was his turn to hum. He kept going faster and faster and listened to El come unglued.

"Coming. Damn...so good. Harder. Mm-m."

He wished he could see El's face. He wanted to see him come undone. *Next time*, he promised himself. He was going to know every inch of El's body.

It wasn't long before El came in his mouth, screaming loudly. The whole complex would probably know what was going on and Remi didn't care.

But he didn't have time to revel in his success. El latched harder onto Remi's cock and sucked him down to his root.

El stopped the blow job to demand, "Flip over."

He didn't waste time turning to be in a better position for El. It was his turn to fall apart. El used his hands to pump Remi's shaft while sucking the very tip. El ran his tongue on the bottom ridge. That was Remi's sweet spot. He hated that he wasn't going to be able to last.

"Your mouth. Fuck, El." Remi threw his head back and did his best not to thrust his hips. He clutched the sheets in his fist to hold himself back.

His balls drew tight to his body and he came faster and harder than he ever had in his life.

El collapsed beside him. He was panting just as hard as Remi was. If this was how good a blow job was between the two of them, he was going to self-destruct when they had sex. Remi threw his arm over his head and did his best to control his breathing.

"Thank you."

Remi raised his head so he could look at El. "I should be thanking you. Wow."

"I'll second that wow." El grinned.

It was nice to see him relaxed. He could see when El remembered why he was there and not at home. His face drained of color and he frowned. Remi couldn't have that. Tonight was about making El feel good, about giving him a few hours of forgetting what was going on in his life. Everything would still be there when he went home. Remi turned to his side and kissed

El's thigh. He was going to work his way back up El's body so he could indulge in kisses.

"What are you doing?" El rose onto his elbows.

Remi didn't answer him. He kissed El's soft cock. It twitched but didn't grow hard. He'd give it time. For now, he just wanted to enjoy his new lover's body. He took the limp dick into his mouth and gently sucked it.

El flopped back down on the bed with a groan. Remi didn't stay there for long. He nipped at El's thighs before moving to his belly. He licked his way up to El's nipples. His body was salty. They'd worked up a sweat in the little amount of time it had taken for them to come. The next time he wanted to take it slow, to see how far he could push El before the man came apart in his arms. Remi flattened his tongue against El's tiny pink nipple. He took turns licking between the two.

"Remi…"

"El…" he murmured against El's skin. He shivered under Remi. "You're delicious. Next time, I'm going to lick you from head to toe."

"I'm getting hard again," El said.

"Good. I want you inside me."

"You say the sweetest things."

Remi nuzzled El's neck, nipping light enough not to leave a mark. He sucked on El's ear lobe, but that wasn't where he wanted to be. He wanted to kiss his lips. Remi nibbled on El's bottom lip before easing the sting with his tongue. If they stayed in bed for a month, that still might not be enough time to find out all the things that made El tick.

"El— Mm-m…" Remi pressed their lips together. El was hard again. Remi took advantage of the situation and rubbed against him while taking his time sipping at El's perfect mouth.

The pleasure surged through him. There was no way he could come again so soon. He didn't think El could either. Remi encouraged El to wrap his legs around him. "Remi—"

"Feels so good."

"Mm-m. More. Harder."

"No."

"No?" El echoed.

"You need to come inside me. If I go any harder, we'll both come before that. I'm not ready."

"You are not being user-friendly."

Remi threw his head back, his laughter bouncing off the walls. He didn't know sex could be so much fun. He was learning so many new things now that he had El in his life. Remi moved over so he could reach his bedside table. There were lube and condoms in there. He'd hoped he could get El back here and that they'd end up in the bedroom. He was hopefully optimistic, and it had worked in his favor.

"I'm about to become *very* user friendly." Remi winked. He grabbed the lube and shook the bottle. He tossed it to the bed and took a condom out of the drawer. He put that on the bed as well.

He arranged himself so El could see his ass. He opened the bottle of lube, put some in his hand and worked it over his fingers before rubbing it into his hole. He eased a finger in. It was good, but not as good as it was going to be. He felt more than saw El move. One of his lover's fingers eased in alongside his. He moaned his delight. El squeezed Remi's ass cheek with his other hand.

"Enough. In me." Remi couldn't wait to feel El's cock in his ass. It had been too long for him and he hadn't ever wanted anyone as much as he wanted El.

"Are you sure?"

"El!"

"Okay, okay." El nipped Remi on the ass before moving into position behind him. "I just don't want to hurt you."

"A little burn is good."

"Mm-m." El ran his hands down Remi's thighs.

Next Remi heard the crinkle of the condom wrapper and the snick of the lube. He turned to look over his shoulder. El was using the lube on himself.

"Ready?" El asked.

The tip of El's dick at his entrance.

"God, yes." Remi hung his head, closed his eyes and waited.

He didn't have long. El eased into him and the burn was a good one. Remi rocked his hips back. He needed him in deeper.

"Slow down. I'm in control here," El told him.

"If I agree with you, will you— Gah!"

El was balls-deep inside him.

"You feel so good, El. Full. Mm-m…"

"Tight. You're so tight. Give me a second." El rested his upper body along Remi's back.

His lover was wrapped close around him.

"You need to move." Remi rocked back.

"I am moving." El stroked his chest and tweaked his nipples.

"Harder."

El didn't listen to him. He pulled almost all the way out before easing back in. It was driving Remi crazy. He tried to slam back onto El, but he couldn't, not with how El was positioned. It was too much and not enough at the same time.

Remi crawled away from El, turned around and pushed him onto the bed. The condom fell off, but that was okay. Remi got another one from the drawer and put it on El's dick before climbing on top of him. He positioned himself so he could get El's cock inside him again.

"No. Fair," El muttered.

"Life's not fair, El." Remi began rocking, and he put his hands on El's chest for balance. "You feel so wonderful inside me."

"Too fast, Remi."

"Not fast enough."

"I'm going to come."

"Good. Do it."

"No, not until you do." El shook his head.

"Nuh-uh."

El grabbed Remi's dick and stroked. "See? You. First."

Remi rocked harder, up and down, racing toward the finish.

"Close?" Remi gasped.

"Mm-m." El closed his eyes and threw his head back.

That was it, he was going to help El finish. He licked his lips and pressed his palms onto El's chest. *Almost. There. Close. So. Close.*

"Remi!" El screamed and came inside Remi.

It triggered Remi's own orgasm. He'd never felt anything so intense. He didn't want to let go of El.

"Thank you," whispered El as he fell onto the bed beside him.

"I should be thanking you. God, El. That was—"

"Amazing."

"Yes, it was."

"Not bad for what started as a fake relationship."

Remi laughed. "I guess not. There was nothing about *this* in the contract."

He looked over at El. He wasn't smiling anymore. *Shit.* He shouldn't have brought up the contract. It had made El think about his mother, and they were here trying to forget. He just wanted to comfort his lover in this time of need, to show him he could be there for him.

"Sorry." El looked over at Remi.

"You have nothing to feel sorry for. Just remember that I'm here for you, no matter what. You need money? You need emotional support? *Anything.* You just need to ask."

"I'm not good at that, you know?"

"I figured as much. I saw how much you struggled with asking for overtime, much less anything else. You're independent. There's nothing wrong with that, but I need you to know that I'm here."

"Thank you. I really do appreciate it."

Remi hoped El would take him up on his help. But even if he didn't, Remi would still be there. He could help from the background if he needed to. He just wished El had come to him sooner. His mom's passing was going to destroy him. Remi wasn't going to let that happen, not on his watch. El was too important to him.

Chapter Eighteen

El didn't want to let the magic of the evening be destroyed by his sadness. And now — guilt. Remi made him feel safe in a way he hadn't known he needed. And the sex wasn't bad either. *Okay, it was wonderful. Awesome. Fantastic.* He couldn't think of any more adjectives at the moment, but if they went another round, he was sure he could come up with others.

"Are you hungry?" Remi's voice shook him out of his thoughts.

"Not really."

"Grab that blanket. I'll get the one in the living room. Follow me."

El didn't want to move, but he did it anyway. He wrapped the blanket around himself and waited to see what Remi had planned. He grabbed a couple of waters and they moved off to the balcony. It was dark, and the stars were out. There were no clouds in the sky. The sound of cars could be heard in the background. There was a police car out there somewhere with the siren going off. He was almost sad that it wasn't a game night. The view of the field was lovely. Of course, he wouldn't have come outside in just a blanket if there had been people on the field. They might not be able to see him and he was fully covered with the blanket, but he would have felt too exposed. Now, it was like they were the only two people in the world.

"I love when it's peaceful out here. There is so much going on in my life that sometimes, when I have the chance, I like to sit out here and just…be. You know?" Remi sat on one of the chairs.

"It is very nice here. It's hard to believe we're in the heart of the city."

"That is why they call it a big city with a small-town feel. We're growing so fast, though. The projects coming up are wonderful. They will bring more people in. I can't wait to see what they do with the river project."

"Let me guess… You're bidding on some stuff?"

Remi laughed. "Yes, I am. Anything I can get my hands into. It keeps us busy and helps the city. I'm all for that. I love Fort Wayne, though not everyone does. A lot of people say there isn't much to do, but they really aren't looking. Broadway at the Embassy? And just imagine when we get those apartments finished. And the Botanical Gardens? We've got that big tattoo convention coming up at the Grand Wayne Center. Plus, we have one of the best zoos around. The new music venue opens up soon."

"I saw a picture of one of our cranes putting the sign up. We made that, didn't we?"

"We did. It's beautiful. I actually have tickets to the grand reopening, if you want to go."

"That would be great. You know, I have always thought about moving away, but…I didn't want to leave Mom." El paused for a moment, thinking about his mom's health, but pushing it back. "Now, I love it here. I think it was just a kid's dream of getting away from where he was born. The older I get, the more I just want to settle in. I mean—I wouldn't mind traveling, but this will always be my home base. I grew up in that house. Did you know that?" El looked over at Remi who shook his head. "Well, I did. It took Mom forever to save up for it. She worked double shifts at the factory to do it. She did the same to get me through college. I took out a couple loans, got a few scholarships, but it was mainly her. She sacrificed so much. But...enough of that. I don't want to talk about it. But, yeah. I like it here."

Remi stroked El's hand, turned it over in his and just held it. The contact was nice.

"You can talk about anything with me, even if it's sad. Promise me you'll let me know what's going on with you? I'm here and I'm not going anywhere."

"Do you think your dad knew?"

"Knew what?" Remi squeezed El's hand.

It was like he knew El was trying hard to change the subject. And he was. This night was about the two of them. Later tonight—or tomorrow—he could think about his mom, talk to Remi about it.

"That you'd find a boyfriend if he just put out an ultimatum?"

Remi threw back his head and laughed. "It would be just like him. He is a crafty old man, but I don't think even he'd guess it was possible. But, I'm happy he did give me the choice. It wasn't that I needed the money. I could live on my salary, but it was the principle of it all. He was forcing me to choose. And if he hadn't told me I needed someone in my life, I wouldn't have propositioned you and ended up here. I like where we are."

Remi smiled, lifted El's hand and kissed his palm. "My dad likes you too. He knows all the employees, for the most part, so he knows a little about you, but once he met you, he was dazzled. But, I'm not surprised. You do the same to me. We haven't spent much time together, but I've enjoyed it."

"Me too. Usually I go to work, come home for lunch, go back to work then head back home. Rinse and repeat. It's been that way for a couple of years. Like I told you, Mom went into remission once. This time, though, her blood was too saturated with something. I don't know everything — well, they told me, but I just understood that she couldn't do chemo anymore — and — Wait. We weren't going to talk about this. I just want to say, it's been nice, the little changes."

"I'm glad. Will you spend the night?"

"I want to. I really do, but I think I should go home. Not quite yet though. I want to enjoy the sky some more — and maybe the company."

"Good. We can go snuggle for a little while. You can tell me your hopes and dreams, what you wanted to be when you grew up. That kind of thing."

"Sounds good to me."

El and Remi sat in silence for a few minutes, the sounds of the city surrounding them. It was the best night he'd had in a really long time.

"We should go inside. It's getting a bit chilly."

"Mm-m. Okay." El shook himself. He'd almost fallen asleep.

"Take my hand." Remi held it out and helped El out of his chair.

El followed him inside and they settled on the couch. Remi put some music on and pulled El close.

"So, what *did* you want to be when you grew up?"

El laughed. "I didn't think you were serious about that."

"I am. I want to get to know you, more than just how hard you work and how much you do for the company. I know you're kind and generous, not to mention caring."

"I don't know about all that."

"You should. What you're doing for your mom? Not many people would do that. They'd have her in the hospital or some facility."

"I couldn't do that to her, Remi. How could I take her out of her home?"

"See? Caring and kind. So, what *did* you want to be?"

"A truck driver. You know those big rigs? I wanted to drive all over the country hauling stuff to wherever, explore the world, visit new places. But that never happened. I haven't really traveled outside Indiana, Ohio and Michigan."

"Interesting. What changed?"

"I'm not sure, to tell you the truth. I got into computers and liked to draw. I heard about different things I could do and how I could create things. I was introduced to AutoCAD in college and enjoyed it. I got my degree and worked in a couple of smaller shops. There was an opening here and I'd heard a lot of good things about the company, so I thought… Why not? The rest is, as you'd say, history. What about you? What did *you* want to be?"

"A painter. Then I wanted to be a writer. After that, a chef. There were so many things I wanted to do. My dad had a few different companies and I started this one after a few years to complement his construction business. It's still creative for me. I get to look at drawings and blueprints, put things together. I like seeing a project from beginning to end. I think the most fun I had was when we made those fire pits. They were so creative. We're working on a desk for the front receptionist with bolts and welds, to show off some of the things we can do. That's going to be fun to design. I'm going to talk to one of the welders so we can get something sketched out."

"That sounds so cool. I can't wait to see the finished product. It's something different from all the other big things we do around the shop. We've got some really creative guys out there."

"We really do. I love the company. It really is like my baby."

"You put your all into everything you do, so I can see that. I don't have a passion like that—at least not one that I've found. The only thing I really want to do different is travel."

"You're still young. There's plenty of time to travel."

El shrugged. He'd love nothing more than to drop everything and explore the world. There was so much out there beyond the Midwest, but it was a pipe dream. He just couldn't afford it at this point in his life and he had a hard time looking that far into the future.

"Maybe. For now, I'm happy here."

"I'm happy you're here too." Remi winked at him.

"If I could, I'd stay in this moment forever, but I can't. I should probably head out, but I don't want to move."

"Just a few more minutes." Remi hugged him close.

"Yeah, a few more minutes sounds like heaven." El closed his eyes and drew in a deep breath. He relaxed as much as he could. He was thinking of his mom and of Remi.

If only they had started fake-dating sooner. He would have loved for his mom to get to know Remi. El had always thought his boss was a good man to work for. The company really helped its employees and the community. Getting to know him on a personal level, he could see the kind of man he was and El liked it. For now, he'd take this little bit of time and savor it. He was warm, comfortable and falling asleep. He let himself drift.

Chapter Nineteen

Remi jerked awake. Darn it, he'd fallen asleep. He'd intended just to watch El for a bit before waking him up so he could go home. They both must have been more tired than they'd thought. He'd wanted to give El more time. He'd always looked so tired lately. But he knew El would be upset that he hadn't made it home.

"El," Remi whispered. "El."

He didn't move. Remi shook his shoulder and it was El's turn to jump up. He actually jumped completely off the couch.

"Huh? What?" El looked around the apartment.

"Not a morning person?" Remi didn't laugh, but it was a close call.

"Hm-m. No. What?" El squinted his eyes.

"It's okay. We fell asleep last night."

"Crap." El ran his hands through his hair.

"Sorry. I was going to wake you up, but I must have drifted off as well."

"No. It's okay. I need…hm-m…"

"I think you might need coffee."

"Yes. And the bathroom?"

Remi pointed El in the correct direction. They were going to need a lot of coffee if El's response was anything to go by. He was cute when he was flustered and had bed-head. Well, more like couch-head. Remi was a little stiff from sleeping on the couch all night. Usually it was comfortable, but he normally didn't have someone sharing it with him. He was surprised they hadn't ended up on the floor at some point.

He was making the coffee when El appeared in the kitchen.

"Thanks for letting me sleep. I think I needed it."

"Are you more awake now?"

"Yeah, it takes a few minutes for my brain to turn on. Coffee does help. What time is it?" El rubbed his eyes.

"It's five a.m."

"Good. That should give me plenty of time to go check on Mom before I head in to work. Oh…and change. I probably shouldn't go in wearing the same thing I wore yesterday. It feels like it's been weeks, not one night."

Remi opened his arms and El walked right into them. "I can't even begin to imagine what you're going through. Watching your mom go through everything? I have no words." Remi squeezed El tight.

"It's been rough. I have cousins, but they don't know how bad it is and I didn't want to burden them. Sara Jo knows everything. We've been friends for so long that I had to tell her. It's nice to have someone else I can talk to."

He let El go and went back to the coffee pot. He poured El a cup before pouring one for himself. They sipped coffee in silence for a moment. Remi could picture the two of them doing this every morning and it scared him. He'd gone from not wanting to date, to seeing a future with someone he'd just technically started dating. Sure, El had worked at the company for a while, but it wasn't the same thing. Before, he had just been an employee and now he was becoming something more.

"I'm happy to be here when you need me," Remi finally said.

"Thank you." El drained the last of his coffee, rinsed out his cup and set it in the sink. "I'm going to run home. Thank you again for last night. I needed the breather. I've been so run down."

"Self-care is important, just as much as looking after your mom," Remi stressed.

"It's just so hard when she is slipping away so fast. God, you probably think the only thing I talk about is my mom."

"She's your whole life. I wouldn't expect anything less."

"Thank you for understanding."

Remi hugged him again. "I'm here for you and I mean it. Now go home. Say hi to your mom for me and I'll see you in a couple of hours."

"Okay. I have to finish up the last part of checking on the entrance to the theater-project apartments today."

"I am going to look at the steel company we are trying to buy later this afternoon. I'm hoping to sign some papers today," Remi said.

"So, we'll be a full-stop shop, huh? We draw it up, fabricate with our own steel mill then the other division erects it."

"It's been a dream for a while to be more self-sufficient. More people want material that is domestic. We'll also have other fabricators buying from us. And if we get their customer list in the sale, we'll have that to add to the company too. I'm going to have to find someone to run it."

"Sara Jo," El said instantly.

"What?"

"She would be great at something like that, plus she knows most of the work from being your admin."

"I'll have to think about that. She does have the skills. And her background lends itself to management. I always thought she was wasting her time as my administrator," Remi said.

"You can move Kiki to be your personal assistant, then you'd just have to find a receptionist."

"You're pretty smart. Has anyone ever told you that?"

"Maybe a time or two." El smirked. "Now, I really have to go. I'll see you soon."

El gave him a hug and a peck on the lips. It was a nice domestic thing for him to do. Just another reason to freak Remi out, but he was taking it in stride. He had to. There was no way he wanted to ruin what they were starting and him freaking out because he was thinking about the future wasn't going to dissuade him from dating El.

He was going to have to talk to his dad. He wanted to be honest with him and thank him. If it hadn't been for him, he never would have asked El out, even if it was supposed to be fake. After he had a shower, maybe he'd ask his dad out for lunch. It was as good a time as any. After, they could check out the steel mill.

Remi stood at the door for a few seconds before going back to the kitchen for another cup of coffee. He had plenty of time before he had to get to work. He thought about the previous night and this morning. Remi didn't make it a habit to have someone stay over, even when he had been actively dating. It just wasn't done. But it had been nice to wake up with El in his arms. Sure, it would have been better if they'd been in bed, but the casual intimacy was something Remi didn't know he'd want. He did, though. He craved it now, and that was only after one night. He was a goner if El stayed over more.

But he couldn't think about that now. It would be selfish of him to take more of El's time. His mom wouldn't be around for much longer. That sucked beyond belief. He wanted to get to know Kathleen more. He wasn't sure if that was going to happen. She'd looked really bad the previous night.

He put his coffee cup in the sink, turned off the coffee maker and headed for the shower. It was time to get ready for the day.

* * * *

When Remi arrived at his office he didn't see El's car anywhere. It was still early, but he hoped everything was okay. For now, he'd get to work. He wanted to call his dad and bring him up-to-date on the plans for the takeover of the steel mill, to get that working as soon as possible. He wanted to know the ins and outs of the new business and that would take a few weeks to work on. He was keeping a lot of the staff, but he wanted some of his own people in there as well. Sara Jo wasn't at her desk yet, but he'd need to remember to talk to her later, to see if she wanted to take over the day-to-day at the mill. He trusted her and El was right, she'd do great at the job.

His phone rang before he could sit down.

"Hello, Marlow here."

"Marlow? I thought it was Remi." The voice on the end was almost a purr.

I'd know that voice anywhere. Why was Harry calling him? It had been— What? Three years?

"Harry. What can I do for you?"

"Have lunch with me."

Remi shook his head. What was Harry playing at? It wasn't like Remi had walked away all those years ago. This was his past calling to haunt him.

"I'm sorry, but I have plans. Did you want something?"

"To talk to you."

"I have no idea why you'd want to do that, Harry. It's been a long time. I don't think we have anything to talk about."

"Aren't you a little curious?"

"Not really. If you don't actually want anything, I need to get back to work."

"It's still early. Surely you have other people who can do...stuff. Just call everything off and come see me."

"You must really not remember who I am. I'm not leaving. I've got a schedule to stick to."

"Fine. Be that way." Harry hung up.

That was the oddest thing that had happened in a while. He put the phone down and went to work. It was a half-hour later when Sara Jo stuck her head in.

"Morning, boss."

"Hey, good morning." Remi set aside the paperwork he was messing with. "Why don't you come in here?"

"Sure." Sara Jo walked into the office and sat in the chair in front of his desk. "What's up?"

"I was talking to El—"

"Oh…really?" She winked at him.

He could feel the heat rushing to his face. "Anyway, we were talking about the steel mill the company is buying and I told him I was going to need someone to run it. He suggested you."

"He… What now?"

"He thought you'd be great for the job and I have to say that I agree. You're qualified from all the years you've worked here. You know how I like things run. There would be a bonus in it for you, as well as a pay raise. I wouldn't just drop you into the situation. You'd be trained, as would I. I know the steel business, but not from the mill side. What do you think?"

"I— But what about you?"

"I'd move Kiki to your job and we'd find a new receptionist. That was El's idea too." Remi smiled.

"Of course it was. He just has an answer to everything, doesn't he?"

"Think about it, Sara Jo. I'm serious. I want you in that position. The mill is in Columbia City, which is closer to where you live. Your commute will be less. I'll be here behind you every step of the way. Do this, for me."

"Let me think about it. It's a big step," she said.

"It is, but I have faith in you. I really do."

"Thank you. I appreciate that, but I enjoy being your second-in-command."

"But just think… You'll have even more people to boss around." Remi winked at her.

"You know you like it when I boss you around."

"Maybe. You'll just have to teach Kiki how to do it right."

Sara Jo laughed. "She'll keep you in your place."

"I'm sure she will."

"I'll let you know tomorrow. I need to make a pros-and-cons lists."

"You and your lists."

"They've saved *you* a few times."

"Well, Sara Jo, you aren't wrong." He had to agree.

"I have some things to take care of, so get back to work," she told him.

"Yes, ma'am." Remi saluted her.

That had felt good. He enjoyed helping others better themselves, and Sara Jo was going to do a wonderful job at the new mill. His appointment wasn't until after lunch, so he had plenty of time to look at some prints for his pet project, the low-cost housing he was going to set up. He was very excited to get that one started, more so than working at the historical site of the Embassy.

Remi gathered the paperwork he'd need for the contract. They lawyers were meeting them at the mill. It was an exciting new step for the company.

His door slammed open. Sara Jo must not have been at her desk because no one usually barged in like they owned the place. But he should have suspected his ex would show up at some point in time.

"Didn't I tell you over the phone that I have nothing to say to you, Harry?"

"I figured you needed to see me in person."

"No, I really didn't. You can leave now. I *really* have nothing to say to you."

"I have some things to say to you — and you're going to listen. Or maybe I'll just show you." Harry circled around Remi's desk, pulled his head down and kissed him.

Remi struggled to get away. He had no idea what Harry thought he was doing, but it was pissing Remi off. There was a loud gasp at the door. Remi managed to push Harry off of him. *Damn it.* He looked and it wasn't Sarah Jo. It was El. He had tears streaming down his face. He turned and walked out.

This can't be happening.

"El! Wait. Please." Remi ran after him.

Harry was talking, but Remi wasn't listening. *That bastard better not have ruined things.* He had just found El and there was no way he was going to lose him.

He managed to get to the front door, but El was gone. Harry was behind him and wrapped his arms around Remi's waist.

"Get the fuck off of me. Leave now and never come back or I'm going to take a restraining order out on you."

"For kissing you? That guy totally overreacted."

"Don't make me tell you again."

"Why are you playing hard to get?"

"I'm not. We've been over for a long time. I don't know what made you think we'd pick back up after all these years. Leave or I'm calling the police."

"You're no fun." Harry turned to leave.

"Don't come back. I mean it."

"Fine. Your money isn't worth all this anyway. I just didn't want someone else getting what was mine."

"Harry, I was never yours. And with a comment like that, I know why."

Sara Jo was at his door when he got back to his office.

"What happened?"

"My ex showed up and thought it would be fun to play tonsil hockey with me, just as El walked in. He ran, I tried to catch him but he was too fast. I need to get him on the phone."

"You need to get to the restaurant. Your dad is waiting then you have the meeting at the steel mill."

"That can wait."

"It really can't, Remi. This has been too long in the making."

"But – El…"

"I'll try to contact him. I'll let him know what went on."

"You believe me, right? That I wouldn't go kissing someone else?"

"I see the way you've been looking at El. I'm going to guess the fake part of the relationship is over." Sara Jo laughed.

"It is. I really like him. I want to see if this will work. I don't want it over before it has even begun."

"Once he's calmed down a little, he'll listen."

"God, I hope so."

"He will. Now *go!*"

"See? You're the boss already."

Remi didn't like leaving things between them like this, but Sara Jo was right. They had been working this deal for months. It was time to get it put to bed. He could have skipped lunch with his dad, but he wanted to come clean with him about what was going on. And he could use some advice.

* * * *

His dad was sitting at their usual table at Hall's Guest House. God, he loved his dad and hoped he wouldn't be pissed as well when he found out what was going on.

"Hey, Dad."

"Hello. You look upset. What's going on?" his dad asked.

"No small talk, huh?"

"Not today. What's wrong?"

"Everything, Dad." Remi sighed.

"Tell me."

"I propositioned El to be my fake boyfriend," Remi admitted.

"I know."

"What?" Remi didn't think he'd heard correctly.

"Do you really think I'd buy the whole 'We've been dating' thing?" his father asked.

"Yes," Remi replied.

"I'm old, not an idiot."

"Then why did you go along with it?"

"You were dating. I didn't care if it was fake. I was hoping it would turn into more," his father explained.

"Well, wish granted. Only… Shit, Dad, I messed up. Harry stopped in. He figured he'd kiss me and who should walk in? El. And it isn't as if he doesn't have enough on his plate. His mom is dying. That was the only reason he agreed to play along. He needed the money."

"You were paying him!?"

"It never got to that. He needed to get her in to an experimental trial that insurance wouldn't cover, but she started going downhill too fast. We haven't gone out much but, we both noticed there was something between us, so we thought we'd try it for real. Now that's all fucked up unless he'll listen to me. I should probably wait until after his mom passes."

"No, you shouldn't. You need to talk to that boy and be there for him."

"I know, but what if he won't listen?"

"Find a way. I like him."

"I like him too, Dad. I never really noticed him before, at least not as a potential boyfriend, but once you made the ultimatum and he came into my office asking for overtime, it fell into place. He's great, Dad. He loves the company, he's sweet and funny and so loyal. He'd do anything for his mom and it sucks so much that she's dying. I wish I could get to know her better, but I don't want to take away from his time with her. She looked really bad. You could tell she'd been sick for a while and she was having trouble breathing. I don't know how much time she has left."

"All you can do is be there for him."

Remi was going to do his best to make sure he was. El *had* to listen to him. *Fuckin' Harry.* Remi put it out of his mind for now. He'd get through the meeting then go to El's house, if he had to. They were going to work this out if it was the last thing he did.

Chapter Twenty

El couldn't breathe. He gasped for air. He'd had to pull over. The tears streaming down his face made driving difficult. What had he just seen in that office? He'd needed Remi. God, did he need him. *My mom. Fuck.*

The day had started off so wonderful. Waking up with Remi was something he didn't think would ever happen to him. He was so used to being on his own. *Damn it.*

But when he'd walked into his house after driving home from Remi's place, he'd seen Susie rushing into his mom's room. The crash of something — Hell, he still had no idea what that had been. It had all been a blur. He'd followed and his mom… *No. It didn't happen. It's a nightmare.* She — He didn't want to think about it. Her gasps for air. She hadn't been able to get any into her lungs. She had been choking. Why hadn't Susie helped her? Someone had to.

He hadn't understood what was happening until she'd stopped moving. He'd yelled at her, shaken her, but there had been no response. Susie had tried to tell him it was okay, that his mom was in a better place. *No. She isn't.* Home was the better place, not her dying. He'd watched her die.

Susie had called Brett, the hospice nurse. He'd come in to check El's mom. It got real when he pronounced his mom dead. She wasn't coming back. He hadn't been prepared for that. Nobody would have been. His heart hurt had so bad that he'd clutched at his chest and wondered if he was having a heart attack. He'd had to find Remi, to tell him what had happened, to get the support he'd promised. But when he'd gone back to the office, the only person El wanted to see, needed to see — the person who'd promised to be there for him — had been lip-locked with some guy.

El kept flashing back to his mom in her bed, her eyes fixed and staring at the ceiling. He'd tried to close them, but that hadn't worked, not like it did in the movies. It was surreal. He was alone in the world. His life had been work and his mom. Now they were both gone.

It took a bit for him to hear the tap on his window. He looked up. There was a police officer standing there. El rolled down his window.

"Sir, are you okay?"

"No."

His short answer seemed to surprise the cop.

"Is there something I can do for you? We got a call from the homeowner that you've been sitting here for a while."

El looked around. He'd stopped a bit before his house. He couldn't believe he'd made it this far.

"Nobody can do anything. I'm sorry."

"Can I take you somewhere?"

"My house is just up there." El pointed ahead of him.

"Are you okay to drive?"

El nodded. "Yes, sir." He really didn't want to go home, though. Reality would hit him again once he walked back into that house. The mortuary had already picked her up. Brett had called them after El had given him the go-ahead. The house would be empty. Brett and Susie had left after his mom had been taken away. They weren't needed anymore.

"All right. If you need anything—" the officer said.

"Thanks." El managed a smile.

The policeman walked back to his car. El couldn't believe he hadn't heard him pull up behind him. And to be caught crying? Well, worse things had happened that day. He started his car back up and drove the minute it took to get to his home. He pulled into the driveway and sat. He didn't want to go in. His life was forever changed.

There were things he had to go through, decisions to be made. *Her will.* She'd had everything ready. She'd tried to tell him, but he hadn't wanted to listen. Now…he had no choice.

El rubbed his chest. He wasn't having a heart attack, but he did have a broken heart. He wondered if he had some booze. He needed to be very drunk. He turned off the car and trudged inside. He dropped the keys on the table and shut the door. The sound echoed around the room. El fell to the floor, cradled his head in his hands and rocked back and forth sobbing.

He had no idea how long he stayed there. Finally, he made himself get up and go to his bedroom. He was done dealing with the world. El took his phone out of his pocket. The message light flashed but he didn't care. There was no way he could talk to Remi. *Tomorrow.* It was another day, after all. *God, mom loved that movie.*

He was going to take Scarlett's advice. Sara Jo… He needed to talk to her…but not now. His heart wasn't working and neither was his brain. The only thing that was functioning were his tear ducts. He couldn't stop. El put his phone with his keys and rushed to the bathroom. He dry-heaved. When he finished, he crawled into the tub—the bed was too far—the cold porcelain nice against his hot skin. The only thing missing was whiskey. Later, he'd drink himself stupid. Now, he needed to close his eyes. She was gone. His mom had left him, and he couldn't do anything about it. He rocked back and forth. The movement should soothe him, but nothing did. Nothing ever would. His heart had been destroyed in a matter of hours.

Fuck it. El wiped his face. He needed oblivion. Rocking in a bathtub wasn't going to do that. He struggled to get out and stumbled to the kitchen. El threw open every cabinet and every drawer in there. It took a few tries, but he found it, an almost-full bottle of whiskey. They'd used it for hot toddies, but now it was going to heal what ailed him.

He opened the bottle and chugged some down. It burned, but he took another drink—and another. The living room couch called to him. He drank a little more.

The burn is good.

* * * *

El blinked. Why was he awake? His head was going to explode. *Am I on the couch?* It took a second for his brain to catch up. The pounding wasn't his head. It was at the front door. He stumbled around until he reached it. He threw it open. Sara Jo was on the other side and it was dark out.

"What time is it?" His words slurred, and he frowned.

Maybe drinking all that alcohol hadn't been the best idea he'd had. El wiped a hand down his face. It was taking everything he had not to cry anymore.

"Nine at night. I've been calling you for hours." She had her hands on her hips and glared at him.

"You have?" El patted his pockets, but his phone wasn't there.

"Where's your mom?"

Oh. God. He...couldn't breathe again. El collapsed to the floor.

"Oh no. El?"

He shook his head. He couldn't say the words out loud. It would be too real. Sara Jo knelt beside him and put her arms around him.

"She— I can't— Damn it." El buried his head into Sara Jo's neck.

This was what he'd needed earlier, but he wasn't going to think about Remi. *One breakdown at a time.*

"Sweetheart, I am *so* sorry." Sara Jo rocked him, running a hand down his back.

The front door was still open. They should close it, but he couldn't make himself. If he could stay in this spot forever, that would make him happy. It was like someone had taken his heart out of his chest, thrown it on the floor and stepped all over it.

"I knew. I knew. I did. But, Sara Jo, she's gone. I can't fix it. I didn't even get to say goodbye. I spent the night with—" That brought on another onslaught of tears. "I got home this morning and—she wasn't breathing right. It was like she couldn't catch her breath. She gasped. Oh, God. What am I going to do?"

"Right now? Nothing. Let me help you to the couch."

Sara Jo shut the door before reaching down to help him off the floor.

"It's so empty. *I'm* so empty."

"I know. It isn't going to magically get better. It's going to take time. It will always hurt a little, no matter how long it's been. Right now, you grieve. That's all you need to worry about. But…maybe no more whiskey?"

"No. You're right. It doesn't help. Not really. It eased the pain and made me sleep, but now it's back and it's just as bad."

"Have you eaten?"

"No, I'm not hungry."

"I'll let that pass for tonight, El, but this can't be an ongoing thing. Don't make yourself sick."

"I have so many things to do, but I don't want to do any of them."

"Let me help you."

"Just you being here helps, Sara Jo."

El was still rocking back and forth. It soothed him for some reason. He couldn't stop himself. He didn't know what to do. He should call the funeral home, get things ready for a funeral. He needed to find the paperwork where his mom indicated what she wanted done. He couldn't remember what he'd done with it.

He was going to have to go into her room. *No. I can't. Not yet.*

The hospital bed they'd rented needed to go back. Not that they'd had it long, his mom had been stubborn about getting it. *Had been.* At this rate, he was never going to stop crying.

"I'll be right back," Sara Jo said.

El didn't want her to leave at all, but he was being selfish. She came back a second later with a bottle of water.

"Drink this, please. You're going to make yourself sick, and you must be dehydrated. Nothing has to be decided tonight, El. And if it did, someone would have called you, I'm sure. So take some time."

He nodded. He didn't have a choice right now. There was no way he could do what he needed to.

"Speaking of your phone, do you even have it?"

"I don't know. Everything has been a blur since this morning."

"Let me look for it." Sara Jo went to the table by the door. "Well, that was easy." She picked up the phone and brought it to him. "You have a ton of texts here and at least one voicemail."

She tossed the phone to him. Their conversation seemed so normal, like his life hadn't been obliterated just hours before. If his eyes weren't tired and probably puffy, he might even let himself believe it. It was just friends as usual. El looked through his phone. He wasn't going to listen to voicemail right now, but he could see who'd texted him. He had missed calls from Sara Jo and…Remi. *Fuck.* The texts were from both of them too. There was one from his supervisor.

Sara Jo looked over his shoulder. "You should read the ones from Remi."

"I can't."

"Nothing happened," she said.

"What do you know?"

"I was there when you stormed out. I saw how devastated Remi was."

"He got caught! Of course he was upset." El threw up his hands.

"That wasn't what happened. You've never met Harry, and be glad you haven't. I've been with the company a long time and the guy is bad news. Remi was better off without him. There is no way he'd get back together with him, not after the way I've seen him this past week. You should talk to him."

"I can't. Not yet. I hurt too much, Sara."

"Fine, but I'm going to tell him your mom died. He's going to want to know."

"If you say so."

"Don't give up so easily, El. You two are good for each other."

El teared up again. It was too much. He couldn't deal. "He hurt me on the worse possible day of my life," he said.

"I know, sweetie. I know. But things aren't always as they appear." Sara Jo hugged him to her and rubbed his arm.

"I just want to sleep and never wake up."

El closed his eyes and drifted off. He wanted to wake up from this nightmare, but life wasn't going to let him.

Chapter Twenty-One

El wasn't answering Remi's calls or texts and neither was Sara Jo. He was going crazy. Had she talked to El? Told him it wasn't what he'd thought? Stupid Harry. Why did he choose now to show back up in his life? It had been out of the blue.

He hadn't gone to work. The middle of the week wasn't the best time to take off and he usually had to approve payroll on Wednesdays, but in his absence, someone else could do it. He should be there, though. That was his life, his baby, but right now all he could think about was if El hated him. They'd just started something that could be special and now it might be all over. That was why he'd stopped dating to begin with. His heart couldn't take it. Harry had broken him at one point. He'd gotten over it and thrown himself into his company.

Now he was hanging around the apartment to figure out what his next step would be. Should he go over to El's house? He didn't want to disturb Kathleen. Was El at work? Did he quit after seeing that stupid kiss? Remi got off his couch and paced. His place wasn't big enough. He had to get out of there. Remi went to his bedroom to throw on some sweats. He was going to go for a run. He needed to do…*something*. Just pacing and sitting around was driving him nuts.

Maybe he should have gone into work. *Maybe I'll do that after running.* Yesterday, the meeting had gone well. The steel mill was now part of the Marlow empire. He hoped Sara Jo would take him up on his offer to run the place. His dad was all for it when they'd talked at lunch. He still needed to talk to Kiki to see if she wanted to be his assistant, but that would come later. He grabbed his phone and some headphones, so he could blast music while he ran. The complex had a gym, but he needed the exertion that only a run would provide. He slipped into his gym shoes and walked out of the door.

He set a fast pace around the block. There weren't many people out. Most of them were probably at work by now. He couldn't wrap his head around the fact that he wasn't at his office, that he was moping over a man and a misunderstanding. He hated not communicating. *People should talk.* And he wanted to do that so bad. God, yesterday had started out so wonderful. Sure, they could have woken up in a bed instead of a couch. He'd had a crick in his neck and his legs had been cramped, but it had been worth it to wake up with El. It was then he'd realized he was happy that they'd called off the fake relationship and decided to actually date.

He had so many plans for El. He wanted to take him to all his favorite places around town and maybe some out of town. He was going to need a distraction when his mom died. Remi needed to be there for him. Sure,

El had Sara Jo, but he needed more. Remi wanted to be that. *Hell, skip wanted*. He needed to be there for him.

Remi turned the music up. He needed to get out of his head for a bit. He passed a few restaurants before going onto a side street. He was starting to breathe hard. He really wasn't in good enough shape to be attempting a run around the city, but he was pushing himself. His stomach cramped, so he had to pause and bend over. He was so out of shape. It was time to do something about that. He stood up, shook his legs before walking to his building. He needed a shower — and work.

He was kidding himself thinking he could stay home and wait for someone to answer his calls. There was nothing he could do right now as much as he wanted to. Sara Jo knew what had happened. She had to have talked to El. The ball was in their court now. He'd called. He'd texted. He could go try to see El in person, but it might be too soon. He wasn't giving up, but he had to be patient.

The bathroom called his name. He might not have run too much, but it was enough to make him sweat. He peeled his clothes off and left a trail into his bathroom. He turned the shower on hot and stood under the water with his palms on the wall and his head hung, letting the water pound into him, relaxing his body. He stayed under until the water went cold.

He toweled off, went to his room and pulled out some clothes. He didn't really care what he wore. He'd thrown his phone on the couch on his way to the shower. He picked it up to see if anyone had responded. They hadn't. With a sigh, he left the comfort of his apartment and headed to work. He could bury his head in the sand there and not think about how his life seemed to be spiraling out of control. Work didn't do that to him. It was a constant in his life, something that wouldn't disappoint him.

The shop had final drawings ready for the theater-project build. The construction part of the company was inside the Embassy and ready to put up the support beams. He drove into work and went right to his office. He had some messages to respond to. His bid on the building for his personal project, the low-cost housing, had been accepted. It was time to start that. Before he knew it, he was buried in work.

* * * *

"Hey, boss." Sara Jo was in his doorway.

Her expression was sad. *That can't be good.*

"How's El?" Remi stood up from behind his desk and headed toward her.

"His mom died yesterday morning. It happened almost as soon as he got home from staying at your place. He needed you after it happened, and when he saw you with another guy, he spiraled out of control. When I got to his place he was drunk. I got him to sleep some."

"I need to —"

"Give him time. He has a lot to do right now. I told him he needed to talk to you and I'm pretty sure he will, but right now his world has fallen apart."

"I'm here for him," Remi said then went back to his desk.

"I know you are. I'll let you know when the funeral is, but, right now, he needs to concentrate on taking care of his mom one last time. After that, he might be ready to listen to you. I know you didn't do anything. I remember what Harry is like."

"I told him I'd get a restraining order if I had to. I don't know why he showed up out of the blue."

"I do."

Remi frowned. "You do?"

"There was an article in the *Journal Gazette* about the Embassy apartments. You were front and center. He had to know it was a great move for the company. He's always been a gold digger."

"God, he totally fucked things up. How do I fix it?"

"I'm in your corner. You know that."

"I do. Thanks, Sara Jo. What am I going to do when you aren't here anymore?"

"What are you talking about?" It was Sara Jo's turn to frown.

"When you take over operation of the steel mill."

Sara Jo held up a hand. "Wait a minute. I never said yes."

"It's just a matter of time. I'll wear you down. I have a meeting with Kiki later today to see if she wants to move up so—"

"Remi…"

"You can do this. And you know I'm here to help. There are some great people at the company already. They'll help too."

"Sure. They won't resent me at all."

"They won't. I am keeping almost all the staff. You'll be directing them. It isn't like you're taking over someone's job. You're just in charge of them all. They know they're lucky. Most takeovers would have the whole staff fired. I'm not doing that. As a matter of fact, I made it a stipulation of the buyout. It's why they went with me. With you overseeing it, it's one less thing I have to worry about. I need to delegate more. El made me see that. I need to spend more time with my dad. And hopefully with El, if he can forgive me."

"Give him some time. The funeral will probably be this weekend. He's trying to get everything in order now. I already let his supervisor know as well. He doesn't have any vacation, but he does have a few bereavement days. He plans on being back to work on Monday."

"That seems too soon." Remi worried his bottom lip.

"Getting back to work will help him, I'm sure. And…yes."

"Yes?"

"I'll take over the mill as the manager."

"Thank you. It takes a weight off my shoulders. It really does. I need to do something, Sara Jo. I can't just sit here and work like nothing has happened. And I shouldn't even be talking to you like this."

"Well—I'm not your assistant anymore and I *am* your friend. We've worked together long enough."

"We have. You need to take the rest of the day off. Go help El. He needs someone, and if it can't be me, it should be you. I'll talk to Kiki. Next week you can train her in the morning and in the afternoon, we'll go to the steel mill so you can get familiar with the operation. By the end of the month, we should be settled. I'll put out an ad today for a new receptionist. Staying busy will help *me,* so that I don't go over to El's and make a scene. I'll take your advice and wait, even though I don't want to. I hate not communicating with him, but I have enough work here to keep me busy. Now go."

There was a knock on the door.

"Hey, guys. Mr. Marlow, you wanted to see me?" It was Kiki.

"Yes, come in. Let me know what I can do, Sara Jo. Anything. Call me. Please."

"I will. Promise."

Sara Jo left and it took Remi a minute to get his head back into work mode. He was worried about El. He hadn't known him personally for long, but he knew how much his mother meant to him. Hell, El had been ready to move in with a virtual stranger to help her. God, he wished he'd been able to help sooner. If he had, maybe Kathleen would still be alive.

"Mr. Marlow?"

"Sorry, Kiki. I asked you in here to have a talk. Please sit down."

"Am I fired?" Kiki twisted her hands together in her lap when she sat.

"What? No! Actually, I asked you in here to see if you'd take over Sara Jo's position as my assistant."

"Is Sara Jo fired?" Kiki bit her lip.

"She is not. She is going to take over another acquisition. The company is now the proud owner of a steel mill. She is going to handle running that. I'm going to move you up to working directly for me and we'll hire a new receptionist. What do you think?"

Kiki relaxed before his eyes. He hadn't realized how tense she'd been.

"Wow. Yes! Are you sure?"

"Of course I am. You've been here long enough and you deserve the change. It will come with a raise, as you'll be doing more work. Sara Jo will help with the transition. And you can ask me anything as you're learning."

"Thank you."

"You are very welcome. We'll start the changeover on Monday."

Remi watched his new assistant leave. It felt good to actually help someone. Too bad it wasn't who he really needed to help.

Chapter Twenty-Two

"Sara Jo, you should go home."

"The checklist isn't done."

El was on the couch sitting across from his best friend. His heart ached, but he was working through it. At least he wasn't in a ball crying anymore. He was drained from the emotion.

"I can finish. I mean, there really isn't much more to do. The funeral arrangements are made. I called the paper for the obituary. I picked the urn. I can't believe she wanted to be cremated." El shook his head.

"You guys never talked about it?"

"I tried to put off talking about this stuff as much as possible. I didn't want to think about it. I don't think she wanted to, either. I mean, we talked about talking." He shrugged.

"All the bills were switched over to my name months ago to make it easier, so I don't have to worry about that. It's just the service, the cremation and the obituary. I didn't know you had to pay to put that in the newspaper. Talk about a shocker. Mom had everything taken care of for the service through the funeral home. I just need to pay for it. Hell, she even had her obituary written out for me. There was a stack of paperwork in her room with my name on it. I went through it before I called the rental place to come get the hospital bed. That's how I made the checklist."

"Didn't she have life insurance to help with some of this?"

"No. She *did* have Disability, which helped some, and insurance helps some, too. That reminds me... I have to let the Disability people know, as well. Is that on the list?"

Sara Jo looked down at the legal pad on the coffee table. "It is, although I think the funeral home does that, but you should verify it with them. And you said that you called the rental company to get the bed?"

"I did. They are picking it up later today. We really didn't have it very long. We probably didn't even need it, but I guess it did help make her comfortable the last few..." God, he was going to cry again. He didn't think he had any more tears to shed.

"Then I think you do have most of it finished. Do you want me to pick up some groceries? Are you having people come over after the service?"

"Yeah, I've made some headway. I'm not having anything after the service. I mean, you can come over if you want, but I really don't think there will be many people there."

Doing the busy work had kept him from thinking of his mom being gone, even though all he was doing was to help send her on her way. It wasn't like she'd really cared about any of this, but she'd tried to make things easier on him. The only people who would probably be there would be him and Sara Jo, along with a handful of her closest friends. He probably hadn't even needed to bother with the obituary.

The viewing would take place on Friday. Saturday there would be a small service and that would be it. Since she was being cremated, they didn't have to go to a cemetery. That would have made it worse, making things too real. He really didn't want to do the showing or viewing, whatever they wanted to call it. He wanted the whole thing over. It was like he was outside himself during the whole process. He wasn't nearly done grieving and didn't think he ever would be. *How does one get over the loss of a parent?* Everyone died. El knew that. He wasn't stupid, but it was never supposed to happen to someone he loved, at least not the someone who'd taken care of him. She'd been there for everything.

When he'd come out, she'd just said, '*I know.*' That had been it. Another day in the household, nothing to see here. When he'd wrecked the car, she'd just wanted to know if he was all right. His mom had been the best. He'd been bullied a little in middle school, and his mom had stormed the principal's office with her LGBTQI-supporting PFLAG group. El had been able to come out pretty early, probably because he was safe with his mom. She'd protected him in every aspect of his life — but he couldn't protect her from cancer.

El put his face in his hands and rocked back and forth. He'd forgotten Sara Jo was there until she came beside him and put her arms around him.

"Shh, I'm here, El. I've got you."

"I thought— It's a nightmare. Why her? God, Sara Jo. She'd been through so much. Why her?"

Now he was getting angry. His mom shouldn't be gone.

"I don't know, El. Your mom? She was a great woman. She loved you with everything she had in her."

"I know. It's just— It's too soon. We should have had more time."

"I know, honey. I know."

They sat there for a few minutes, neither of them talking. The anger drained out of him. He couldn't be upset with his mother. But *fuck cancer*. He moved out of Sara Jo's arms, wiped his face and stood up. He couldn't sit there anymore. He just couldn't. He needed out of the house. There were too many memories there.

"El, this isn't something that is going away after a day or two. It can sneak up on you too. Let it. Don't bottle this up. Remember that I'm here for you. So is Remi."

El barked a laugh. "Right."

"Have you read any of his texts? Listened to his voicemails?"

He shook his head. He couldn't bring himself to look. He was too weak. What if Remi had told him they were done? That he was back with his ex? That they shouldn't be together? He couldn't handle that in his current state. Maybe after the funeral was over and he got back to work...

Fuck. He didn't want to go back and face Remi. How could he work for the guy after everything?

"I won't push you, El, but you should think about contacting him. He's a mess."

"*He's* a mess?" El glared at Sara Jo.

"Yes. And I'll leave it at that."

"You really should go home. I'll see you Friday at the funeral home."

"Are you sure you're going to be all right?"

"No, I won't. I'm not sure if I'll ever be okay again. I'll try, but everything is raw right now. I fucking cry at the drop of a hat. I'm not sure how I'm going to get through Friday and Saturday."

"You're stronger than you think. I know you are. I wish you could believe in yourself. Just remember that it won't go away in a flash. It's going to hurt, but you need to lean on your support. That's me." Sara Jo walked over to him and kissed his cheek. "I love you — and thank you."

"For what?" El wrinkled his forehead.

"Suggesting me for the steel-mill job. I never would have gone after it on my own."

El hugged her. "You're going to do great. I'm just going to miss seeing you every day."

"We can still do lunches sometimes, now that —" Sara Jo looked down at the floor.

"Yeah, now that my mom isn't here."

"I didn't mean —"

"I'm a crying mess, but you don't have to tiptoe around me."

"Okay. Make sure you eat something, El." Sara Jo turned to leave.

"I will," he lied. There was no way he could eat anything. His stomach churned. If he ate anything, he'd throw it up. It wasn't worth the effort.

"If you don't, I'll be back here. Don't make yourself sick."

"I'll see you soon. Bye, Sara."

She nodded before she walked out the door.

The quiet of the place was what got to him the most. His mom's shows weren't on. There was no music. She wasn't shuffling around. He didn't have to cook for her. He walked over to the mantle. There were pictures all over. He picked up an old one of them at Christmas when he was…maybe five. She seemed happy.

Everything in the place reminded him of her. He waited a few minutes to make sure Sara Jo was really gone before heading out. He needed the fresh air. El took his keys to lock up, but he had no plans to drive. Walking would do him good. His phone buzzed in his pocket but, for now, he ignored it.

Night would be there soon. It was a bit chilly, but he didn't care. A couple of blocks later, he took his phone out of his pocket. There was no way he could listen to the voicemails. It would hurt to hear Remi's voice, but he could read the texts. There were a few. He scrolled back to see if he could find the first one. He stopped walking. Most of them just said 'sorry' and that Remi could explain, for El to call him.

But I can't, not yet. He wanted to get over one emotional hurdle before tackling another. If Sara Jo believed Remi, he should too. She wouldn't lie to him, but he needed time and space to think. Maybe he wasn't ready for a relationship. Right now, his head wasn't in the game.

El sat down on the curb. He wanted to lie down, but that wouldn't be the best idea. Someone would likely call the cops on him, like they had before. He was drained, done for the night, but he didn't want to go home. He could go see Remi, let him explain in person, but he didn't want to do that either.

With a sigh, El got back up and turned around to walk back to his house, the only home he'd really known. He'd sleep there tonight because he really couldn't afford to stay in a hotel. The bills from his mom's illness and passing would start to come in soon. He was out of overtime, vacation and sick time. Maybe he'd get that second job he'd thought about while his mom had been sick. He hadn't been able to do it then because he'd wanted to spend every available second with her, but he had no one and nothing to stop him now. He could spend his time making sure he didn't lose everything because of medical expenses.

The house came into view. El stopped to stare at it. It wasn't spectacular, a plain white house with black shutters and steps leading up to the door. There was a patio on the back. He'd spent a whole summer building that a few years before. His blood, sweat and tears were in the place. He'd lost his mom. He couldn't lose the house too. That would break him.

He could hear his mom in his head, telling him to let go of the house, to travel, to listen to Remi and fix things. El looked down at his phone. He had an urge to call Remi, but he didn't let himself. He walked into his house then put his keys and phone on the table. He fell onto the couch, face first. He could stay that way until Friday. There was nothing left for him to do but show up at the funeral home. A knock at the door startled him.

He remembered...*the bed*. They were there to pick it up. It was a good thing he'd come back when he had.

There was no more adulting to do after that, so he was done. Maybe he could sleep until Friday. And when he woke up maybe it would all have been a nightmare.

Because...that would happen.

Chapter Twenty-Three

Remi stood in the back of the room. He was doing his best to stay out of the way and in the shadows. As much as he'd wanted to go to the viewing on Friday, Remi had decided to wait to pay his respects until Saturday. His dad had advised him to go over to El's house and hash things out, because life was too short. Remi knew that all too well, but he also knew El needed time. Everything was too fresh.

He was happy Sara Jo had kept him in the loop as to the arrangements. She was in his corner, but above all, Sara Jo was El's friend and just his employee.

For now, El was too focused on the front of the room. He hadn't spotted Remi yet. El seemed fragile all by himself next to the coffin. It was all Remi could do not to go up there and take El into his arms for comfort. Hopefully, there would be time for that later. *God, I hope so.* Despite the fact that things were still new between them, he wanted to be there, but it had to be on El's terms. He'd lost so much already.

"What are you doing back here?" Sara Jo whispered into his ear.

"I don't want to be in the way. Plus, we haven't talked yet, and I don't want to upset him. I won't stay long. I just had to see him for myself. He's so sad."

"He is, but it will get better…slowly."

Remi nodded. "There aren't many people here. I was expecting more."

"He put the obituary in the paper. Kathleen didn't have many friends toward the end. People don't like to be reminded how short life can be."

"That's bullshit." Remi crossed his arms.

"Agreed. We sent a donation to the American Cancer Society in Kathleen's name, as well as some flowers. I figured I'd just do it before Kiki took over."

"Thank you. I sent some from me and Dad too. I wish I could do more."

"You're here. That's something."

"I'm going to leave before he sees me. I'm going to go see my dad and hug him."

El chose that moment to turn around. Remi met his eyes and took a step forward before he remembered himself. He was there for support, not to interfere. Remi gave him a small nod before turning back.

"You should stay."

"He's so vulnerable. I'm not going to take advantage of that. I can let him know I'm here for him when he's ready, but El is going to have to make the call to see me." Remi frowned.

He looked over his shoulder. El was frozen to his spot. It was time for him to leave. Remi hadn't been lying about going to see his dad. He needed his own pick-me-up. It hurt him to see El in so much pain but he didn't want to do something he'd regret, like race up to him, pull him into his arms and kiss him—or just hold him.

One night with El had ruined him, that was for sure. He wanted to take that moment and stop time, the two of them waking up on the couch, saying good morning and living in that one moment for the rest of their lives. But it wasn't a fairytale. Real life hurt. He was living proof.

Harry had tried to call him again. Remi had answered once and told him he wasn't kidding about the restraining order then he'd blocked Harry's number. He didn't want to be someone's sugar daddy. He wanted to be loved for himself. To be honest, he wanted what his parents had had, and he wasn't going to settle for anything less.

Is El the one? Remi hoped so, but time would tell. They could be over before they'd even begun, thanks to his asshole of an ex.

Remi left the funeral home. He knew there would be no graveside service. If there had been one, he would have stayed. Sara Jo wouldn't leave El's side. That was the only way Remi could allow himself to walk out.

The trip to his dad's took longer than usual. Remi took his time, driving around Fort Wayne first. His dad lived out in New Haven, where there was more open space. He actually lived on a farm, so he didn't have any close neighbors. On the other side of his street there was an addition full of people, but it was fairly quiet on his dad's side. Remi had poured his heart out to his father about the misunderstanding with El about Harry. His father would understand, and right now he needed someone who would.

Maybe Remi would stay with his dad a few days. Or, he could go home to his apartment and drink himself silly. That could work too. It hurt not being there for El.

It crushed his heart to think they might never be together again in any other capacity than employee to employer. But if that was how El wanted things, Remi wasn't going to push. Not now. Maybe in a few months, though. He wasn't going to give up, not yet. He would hold onto the hope that El would turn to him. Remi would be ready with open arms.

He pulled into his father's driveway. The groundskeeper was mowing the lawn and the cook had pulled in right before Remi did and was leaving his car. His dad wasn't alone. He had people around him all the time, but that didn't mean he wasn't lonely. Remi had often asked him if he'd ever find someone to live his life with again and he'd always been told that his mom had been his father's one true love and he couldn't do any better than that.

Remi needed to get out of the funk he found himself steeped in or it'd be a one-way ticket to the whiskey bottle. He'd be one drunk-dial away from making a fool of himself. He walked to the front door and walked in.

"Dad," he called.

"In here, Remi."

He followed the sound of his dad's voice.

"What brings you all the way out here?" his father asked.

"El's mom died." Remi sat down next to his dad on the couch.

"Oh no. Did you make up?"

Remi shook his head. "No." He sighed. "I went to the funeral home but didn't talk to him. Not yet. God, Dad, I wanted to go up to him, hug him and never let him go."

"Why didn't you?"

"He wasn't ready. It was all too much. I didn't want to hurt him more. It has to be on his terms. I just wanted him to know I was there if he needed me."

Jackson patted Remi's thigh. "If that's all you can do, at least you did it. I'm sorry to hear about his mother, though. I was hoping for a chance to meet her."

"He loved her so much, Dad. I had to come here and let you know how much I love you. I'm so happy you're in my life. It could have gone another way when I came out, but you've always been there for me when I needed you. When Mom died, I thought we'd go with her, but together we've survived. We have a great company with wonderful employees. *We* did that. I don't want there to be a time we aren't in each other's lives." Remi turned to hug his dad.

"I love you too, kid. It's why I always want what's best for you."

"I know. I shouldn't fight you on things."

Jackson laughed. "You wouldn't be you if you didn't. You have *always* been headstrong. I remember one time your mom was trying to change your diaper. You were having nothing to do with it. You got up off the floor, pulled off your diaper yourself, threw it at her and ran. I caught up with you on the front porch. You were making a run for it, naked as the day you were born."

"You're making that up!"

"I am not. Your mother was too stunned to move. She sat there with the diaper in her hand, watching you run away. It was a good thing it was just pee. God, that would have been a mess."

Remi laughed. It was the first time he'd felt good in days. "Thanks, Dad."

"Any time. I have a lot of those stories stored up. Can I get you something to drink?" Jackson stood and headed to the kitchen.

"I can get it." Remi stood to follow him.

"I've got beer, wine, water— I think there's some diet pop in there too, if I didn't finish it."

"Water sounds good." Remi went to the fridge and pulled one out.

"Grab me one too."

Remi handed a water to his dad.

"I can have the cook make us some dinner or call the pizza place. I have them on speed dial. I think they know who I am."

"I'm not really hungry."

"How are things going at work?"

"Well, as you know, we own the steel mill now. I'm having Sara Jo take over the management."

"I remember us talking about that. It's a good call. She's a smart woman."

"She is. She knows how we run things. It's a good fit."

"I plan on retiring next year."

"What? This is the first you've said anything about retiring."

"I know. I was going to wait, but it's time. I want to go play golf, maybe head down to Florida for a bit…or Arizona, do some traveling, spoil my grandkids when they get here."

Remi snorted. "Way to slide kids into the conversation. So who are we getting to run the construction division?"

"We have a couple of guys who can step up. But they will just be managing it, like Sara Jo with the steel mill. You'll be head of it all."

Remi sat down at the kitchen table. "That's…a lot."

"It is, but I think you need to find a manager for the fabrication division, delegate more so you aren't tied to the business like I've always been."

"Right now, I need the work. It's all I have."

"It isn't. You need to have faith."

"I wish I had your perspective. My relationship could be over before it really began. And now — having three companies to take care of? It seems like too much."

"I'm not leaving for another year — and it isn't like you can't call me if you have an issue. I'm going to have you look at some people in the construction part of the company to help me pick a manager, someone you'll want to work with. I suggest you start looking at some people in your company for taking over more of your job. That will give you time to oversee the three companies. Or — we can sell the whole thing."

"What!" Remi stood up. "I can't believe you'd even suggest that."

"We don't need the money, son. You could travel more, have a personal life. I don't want you to bury yourself in the company. It would be so easy for you to live at that office. Let me help you delegate."

"I'll think about getting a manager for the fabrication part of the company, but I'm *not* selling."

"Okay." Jackson smiled at him.

"Was that a test?" Remi pointed a finger at his dad.

"No. I just know my son. I figured it would get a rise out of you."

"You suck."

"Maybe, but you love me."

Remi sighed. "Yes. Yes, I do."

There was a knock on the door.

"I wonder who that could be?" Jackson asked.

"You aren't expecting anyone?"

"Nope. I wasn't even expecting you." Jackson left the kitchen.

Remi followed along to see who was there.

"Well, hello there, son. I didn't expect to see you here," his dad told the caller.

Remi stood frozen with surprise.

"I'm sorry to interrupt your Saturday, but Sara Jo said Remi might be here, and she gave me your address. I hope that's all right." El bit his lip.

He looked nervous. *God, I want to hug him.*

"Come in."

"Thank you. I just needed to talk to Remi."

"He can take you into the kitchen. I need to go water the plants out back." Jackson winked at Remi.

Way to be subtle, Dad.

Remi led the way to the kitchen with hopes of the future in his heart.

Chapter Twenty-Four

El didn't want to be at this farm. He wanted to go home, hide under the covers and never leave his house. That wasn't going to happen, at least not yet. He needed to get his mom's stuff together, figure out the bills, see what he needed to donate and what had to be thrown away. After all that, he'd have to go back to work on Monday. He couldn't afford to take any more time. His bereavement leave was up, as of Friday. Three days… It didn't seem like enough to say goodbye to someone who had been his whole world since he'd been a little boy.

"Can I get you something to drink?" Remi interrupted his thoughts.

It was a good thing, because he would probably spiral out of control if he kept thinking.

"No. I—uh… I'm not staying long."

"Oh. Okay."

Remi seemed disappointed. El hated the look on Remi's face—the one he'd put there. El bit his lip again. He was a sort of nervous. He shouldn't be. What he should be was upset. He'd caught Remi kissing some guy. It didn't matter that Sara Jo had told him it had meant nothing. On top of his mother's death to see the man he could fall for in someone else's arms had been too much. It still hurt.

"I wanted to say thank you." At least he'd gotten that bit out. "I didn't expect you to show up today or to receive the flowers. They were nice. So was the donation in my mom's name." El wiped a hand down his face.

This was more difficult than he'd thought it would be, not that he'd thought it'd be a piece of cake. Talking to people was hard for him on a good day. Today, he'd said the final goodbye to his mom. *Fuck.* Yeah, he didn't want to go there. He couldn't. Not yet. Because if he thought of his mom not being whole anymore, he *would* break down, right there in front of Remi. He wasn't going to share that. It was for when he was alone at home. Once he got back there, he could fall apart. He still had Sunday to pull himself back together.

"I wanted you to know that I'm here for you, but I don't want to push. Here… Sit down."

Remi pulled out a kitchen chair. El figured he'd better go ahead and sit. If he didn't, he might fall down anyway. If he fell, he wasn't getting back up.

"That's why I'm here." El rubbed his hands on his slacks.

"I pushed?" Remi's brows turned down and a frown graced his lips.

"No." El waved a hand at him. "No. You didn't. But…I need time."

"Off work?" Remi said in a whisper, like he knew that wasn't the case.

"I'll be at work on Monday. From... God, this is going to sound bad. Time...from you. I can't think about a relationship right now. I have to figure out what I'm doing."

"I see." Remi sat down across from him, his eyes downcast.

He wanted to yell at Remi to look at him, but he didn't have that right, not after telling Remi he needed space away from him. How was that even going to work on Monday? El would find a way. He had to. The less he saw of Remi right now, the better, even if his heart was shattering.

El missed the smile and the twinkle in Remi's eyes. Had it only been a couple of weeks? Why did it hurt so bad? He should be able to walk away and be okay, but he wasn't. Would he ever be okay again? They say time heals all wounds, but maybe they got that wrong.

"It— It hurts, Remi."

"You have to know... I didn't kiss Harry. He forced the kiss on me. He was trying to get me back. He'd called earlier that day. I told him then that I wanted nothing to do with him. Then he showed up out of the blue. That kiss? I was trying to get out of it when you walked in."

"Sara Jo told me. It still hurts. And, quite frankly, I'm not sure I'm ready to put myself out there right now. It's...too much, too soon. Everything hit me at once. My mom, you... And I *know* you didn't initiate that kiss. I've worked for your company for a long time. I've seen how you interact with people, how honest and thoughtful you are. We were just starting. You wouldn't jeopardize that. But— I just— I can't."

"I'm not going to lie. It hurts me too. I want to help you and be there for you, but if you need me to step back, I will. Just know that I *am* here for you. Let me know what you need. I'm sure I'll see you at work."

That was a dismissal. It shouldn't hurt, since El was the one asking for the space. He was...empty. El stood and turned from the kitchen.

"I just have to do one thing. Okay?" Remi moved closer, turned El around and pulled him into his arms.

El buried his face into Remi's shoulder. He took a deep breath, inhaling Remi's scent. It was comforting. All he wanted to do was crumple into Remi and let him support him, but he couldn't. That pain was still raw. Even though Remi hadn't hurt him on purpose, it was still there and he'd rather leave Remi than wait for Remi to leave him. He wouldn't survive another heartbreak right then.

Reluctantly, he moved away from the hug.

"Bye, Remi." He turned and raced out of the house.

It had been a mistake to stop at Remi's dad's house. He should have sent a thank you note or something. But, no, he'd wanted to talk to Remi face-to-face after not answering his texts or calls. He owed it to him. El got into his car and drove off without a backward glance.

* * * *

The first thing he did when he got home was change out of his suit. He hated the thing and might burn it. He never wanted to see it again. It would be too much of a reminder of what had happened today. After Remi had left the funeral home, the director had told them they were ready to do the cremation. They would let El know when her ashes were ready. *Fuck. What am I going to do with those?* She didn't have anything written for him, saying where she wanted to be put to rest.

Travel. She'd wanted to go around the globe. He was going to pick a place to spread her ashes. That had been her one regret and he was going to make sure it didn't follow her into the afterlife. El would take her with him to a few places and find a spot to leave her.

But that was something that would have to wait. He didn't have any more vacation time until the next year. It would also give him time to plan. For now, he had bills to look at. He didn't have his mother's final medical bills yet but he knew that insurance wouldn't cover everything. He'd already had to finish paying off the funeral home. His mother had made a deposit to get things going but it had taken most of his savings to take care of that bill. God, he hoped the medical bills could be worked out with some kind of payment plan. He'd heard horror stories of people going bankrupt from medical expenses. El was out of his depth.

When the cancer had come back, his mom had signed the house over to him.

Did he have to do anything now? *No.* He was going to take a shower, change into something a bit more comfortable and make dinner. He wasn't hungry, but if he didn't eat something, he was going to get sick. He kicked his shoes off so he could lose the pants and left a trail of clothing from the living room to the bathroom. There was no one there to scold him. Only silence followed him. He couldn't shake it off. He couldn't remember a time when his mom hadn't had the television on some show she'd tried to get him to watch. Maybe he should have flipped it on before his shower, but he wasn't going back out there.

He reached the shower and turned it on. Once it was warm, he stepped inside. El let the water pound over him. He closed his eyes and couldn't stop the tears from flowing. His shoulders shook, the sobs racking his body. He wanted Remi, but…he just couldn't. What if Remi broke his heart? Where would he be then?

Right where you are now, asshole.

El stayed under the spray until the cold water forced him out. He thought he was cried out, but it hit him again out of the blue. He sighed, the sound echoing around the room. He really needed some noise.

The towel wasn't where it should have been. He remembered taking it to his room that morning. He must not have put it back. He was going to have to walk through the house, cold, naked and wet. It didn't matter. No one was there. No one ever would be.

God, he needed to stop depressing himself. It wasn't doing any good and neither was the crying. *Food.* He needed to eat something. *Clothes first. Maybe. Who cares?* He didn't.

Fuck it.

El changed his course and walked, naked, through the house and into the kitchen. The curtains were open but he had zero fucks to give. He was going to eat something now. He opened the fridge and saw a big bowl of broth. It broke him. No matter how much he didn't want to cry, he was a faucet.

He screamed, grabbed the bowl and threw it into the sink. His mom's favorite drink was next to get tossed. He threw a glass container and it shattered over the floor. There wasn't enough stuff in the fridge. He turned then threw a chair across the room. El leaned forward and slammed the fridge door shut. It bounced back and hit his chest, causing him to fall on his ass, his foot landing in the glass.

"Fuck!"

El couldn't catch his breath. Anger filled him. The screaming and throwing shit didn't help. He wanted to hit something, but his energy had drained out of him, the adrenaline gone. His foot hurt. He should get up off the floor but he couldn't.

Today had been too much, but this was his new life now. There was a big hole in his heart. Nothing could have prepared him for the gaping emptiness in his very soul.

He used the fridge to help himself get off the floor and looked at the mess around him. He wasn't going to do anything about it now. El checked his foot, but didn't see any glass stuck there. His hunger was gone too, so he was going to bed.

El limped out of the room, leaving droplets of a blood trail on the floor, and went to his bedroom. Not bothering with clothes or his aching bloody foot — other than to wrap a towel around it — he dropped onto his bed, pulled the covers over his head and closed his eyes.

He'd start over tomorrow. Maybe the ache wouldn't be as bad. He could always hope for the best. That's what his mom would have done. He took one deep breath, then another and one more for good measure. The anger was gone, but the sadness lingered.

Tomorrow. Yes, tomorrow would be soon enough to deal with his new life. He'd have to get himself together, because Monday would be there before he knew it and he'd have to deal with people — and Remi. El cried himself to sleep, thinking of all he'd lost.

Chapter Twenty-Five

Remi didn't stay long at his dad's after El had left. There had been no need to bum his dad out. While he understood that El needed time, it didn't make his heart hurt any less. His mom had just died and things had to be crazy. Remi felt bad being upset. It seemed selfish.

He unlocked his door and walked into the dark apartment. Remi didn't bother turning lights on, just went toward the kitchen. The keys in his hands dug into his palm as he tried to open the fridge. He shook out his hand, tossed the keys onto the counter and tried once again. He had no idea what he was looking for.

I'm lost. How can this be happening?

What he wanted wasn't in the kitchen. Remi walked aimlessly around the apartment. It was Saturday. He could go out, but going to a club didn't appeal to him. He should eat, but that wasn't going to happen either. There was a game going on. Remi went out to his balcony. It was noisy, but the sound helped drown out the thoughts bouncing around his head.

Like how sad Monday is going to be. Maybe he should call in sick. He was the boss. He could delegate, but he wouldn't. He was also an adult. From the beginning, he'd told El they would be able to go back to a boss-employee relationship after the fake boyfriend contract had expired. He had to stand by that, even if they'd never gotten around to signing anything, even if they'd started to actually date. His heart was invested, but he needed to respect El's wishes. It wasn't like they saw each other every day. They could go months without direct contact. He wasn't El's immediate supervisor. Plus he had appointments around the city during the next week. He wanted to do another inspection on the Embassy apartment project and there was another theater opening back up. He wanted to see if they could bid on that. He wanted to get his pet low-cost housing project underway as well. There was plenty to keep his mind occupied.

None of that helped, though. His thoughts kept circling back to El. He needed to help him in any way he could. It sucked that the only way he could do that was to keep his distance. Life happened. He had to push forward.

The game didn't keep his attention, not like it usually would. Remi headed back inside. He needed a drink—or ten. But, for now, he'd settle for mindless television and a pizza. Comfort food.

He placed the order, turned on the TV and proceeded to flip through channels. Something mindless was on the menu but nothing looked good. Remi finally went to his cabinet of DVDs and selected his favorite, *Hot Fuzz*. That should get him through anything.

Dominos was right down the street, so it didn't take long for his food to get there. The knock on the door startled him. He'd been standing there holding his movie for — He didn't know how long. He had to get over this. It wasn't like he'd been dating El for years. He shouldn't be this invested in something that never was, even if he thought of what could have been. He wasn't one to fantasize about the future.

The pizza was nice and hot when he put it on the table. He needed something to drink so he grabbed a water from of the kitchen, made his way back to the living room and finally put the movie in.

Blankets!

Remi's next stop was the bedroom. He took his clothes off then got into some sweats and a T-shirt. Blankets were next. He was finally ready to settle in for the night. He curled up on the couch, put the pizza beside him and dug in. He could quote the movie by heart and he did. Remi even managed to laugh a couple times. It didn't matter how many times he'd seen the film. He should watch *Paul* next. Maybe even watch some *Shaun of the Dead*.

Before he knew it, the pizza was gone, the movie over and he was right back where he started.

"Fuck." Remi ran a hand down his face.

It was going to take time to get back to normal. That was all there was to it. If he acknowledged that fact, maybe he would stop hurting. He wasn't one to give up, but he didn't want to push. El was too fragile. He'd lost the one person who meant everything to him. Remi remembered losing his mom, but the difference was, he'd had his dad in his corner. He should get his dad to talk to El, maybe take him under his wing. Remi didn't have to be involved.

After a bit of time, Remi could check in and see if El wanted to start again. God, he hoped so. Until then, he was back to work being his only outlet. There were more projects in town he could bid on to keep the work coming in. As a matter of fact, besides the new theater opening back up, he'd just heard they were going forward on the downtown river project. Marlow could build the handrail needed in that section.

Work never failed him. It was his constant, and he'd bury himself in it if he needed to. Anything to help him not interfere—yet. Marlows weren't quitters and he wasn't about to start now. Tomorrow he'd call his dad and see if he'd check in with El. For now, he was going to bed. He could fall asleep to another mindless movie. Maybe something with superheroes this time. Eye candy and explosions were an awesome combination. He wondered what El was up to, if he'd gone to bed yet or if he was pacing around his empty house. Remi grabbed his phone off the table and looked at it. He could call, but he wasn't going to. El had asked him for space. He was going to give it him, no matter the cost to him.

* * * *

Most Mondays didn't suck for Remi, but today was an exception. For most of his life he'd thought of the beginning of the week as a fresh start. Good things could happen, but not this week. And the weekend had seemed to fly by for Remi, probably because he wasn't looking forward to being in the same building as El and not be able to talk to him. Sara Jo wasn't going to be there. She was at their new steel mill. Kiki was starting and there'd be some on-the-job training. At least that would keep him busy.

He should do a staff meeting, but he was putting it off and that wasn't good. He had a job to do in a company he loved. Remi needed to be an adult and do what he'd promised El he'd do. He had to keep it a good work environment.

"Kiki?" Remi called her at her desk.

He could have gone out there, but there was only so much he could force himself to do. If he could, he'd hide out, but he had an appointment at eleven.

"Yes, sir?"

"Remi, please. Would you send out a memo to all the staff? We'll have a staff meeting in the conference room after lunch. Say…two o'clock."

"Yes, sir. Um… Remi."

One thing down. Of course, it was only nine o'clock, two hours before he could leave. He was going to meet with the city planner and see what he could quote on the new riverfront project. They'd been planning it for years and it was finally coming together. It was a good time to be living in Fort Wayne. It still felt like a small town, but they were growing by leaps and bounds. People might complain there weren't things to do, but Fort Wayne had a lot to offer. It was one of the reasons he'd never left. A few years ago, when the economy had tanked, he had been afraid that they would lose the company, but thanks to some good investments and their reputation, they'd kept the doors opened. The employees they'd had to lay off all got hired back. That had been a good day for him.

And I can make more good days. He needed to take it a day at a time. If he happened to be looking forward to the staff meeting so he could see El, he wasn't telling anyone.

The day passed by and it was finally time for the staff meeting. He got there first and waited for everyone to filter in. Remi was beginning to think El wouldn't be there, but he eventually made his way there. He was one of the last stragglers.

"Good afternoon, everyone. We've had a couple changes, so I figured the easiest way to pass it on was to have a meeting. As you know, we started work on the Embassy job. Soon we'll be working on an apartment project that will benefit the community, and I've had a meeting with the people involved in the riverfront project."

A few people clapped. It was a good thing to keep everyone busy.

"The other thing I have to announce is that Sara Jo is moving over to the new steel mill. I'm not sure if you are all aware of the fact that it was purchased. It was a step up for her and I'm sure she'll do a wonderful job. Most of you know Kiki." Remi pointed to his new assistant. She waved at the guys. "She is now my administrative assistant. We have a temp at the reception desk, to see if she is a good fit."

The whole time he spoke, he looked often at El. El looked sad and like he hadn't slept in a week. The urge to hug him was strong, but he kept focus on the people, the ones who counted on him for a paycheck

"If anyone has any questions or suggestions, my door is always open. Just let Kiki know and she'll get you in to see me. If no one has any questions, we'll get back to work."

Remi waited a few seconds, looked around the room, but no one seemed to have anything for him.

"All right then, back at it." He smiled while he said it.

El was the first to bolt out of the room. It was like he couldn't stand to be in the same place as he was. Remi had to sit down. It was as if a physical blow had struck him in the chest. It was a good thing everyone had left. He needed to go home. There were no more appointments that day. He had some paperwork to do, but he couldn't be in his office any longer. He stood up, went to find Kiki and let her know he was leaving. She could call him if she needed to.

After that, he was out of there. The drive home was a blur. He'd stopped off at the liquor store. He had plans to get good and smashed.

The apartment was cold when he arrived, not that that bothered him. He'd be warm soon. Remi didn't even bother to change his clothes. He took one of the bottles of Jack with him to the couch. Not bothering with a glass, he took a giant gulp. It burned, but that didn't matter either. He took another drink—and another. He wanted to be at the point where he could feel no pain. El? El, who? That was the mindset he needed, and the Jack would help him get there.

After one more drink, he slid down to the floor and laid his head back on the couch. He only moved to take another drink. It wasn't hitting him yet, but if he drank enough, he wouldn't remember his own name. That was the state he needed to be in. For how long he didn't know, but today it was drink until he passed out and didn't feel anything. It would be the best day—even if he wasn't going to remember it.

Chapter Twenty-Six

The week sucked and that might be an understatement. Work was…well, work. It helped El get through the days. The nights were the worst. They brought to reality how really alone he was. Now the weekend was there and he didn't want to stay cooped up in the house. He needed to go through his mom's stuff, see what he could donate and what he wanted to keep.

After seeing Remi on Monday, he'd done his best to stay in his office. It had worked. Remi was obviously sad. During the whole staff meeting, El could feel Remi's eyes on him, but he'd refused to look up. *Why can't I just let Remi hold me?* He was keeping them apart when he didn't need to.

What he did need to do was to get his mom's affairs in order. Once that was done? Well, he could see if he and Remi could start something. If they had a connection, it would last until El could come to Remi as a whole man. As a couple, they were too new for El to give Remi his shell of a self.

It was a good thing he had a lunch date with Sara Jo. They could talk about her new job and how that was going. He could put off going through his mom's things for another day. If he could, he'd be working overtime, but he already knew that wasn't an option. Hell, maybe he'd just work off the clock, anything to keep his mind occupied. Thinking about overtime had him thinking about Remi and the one time they'd been together. He wanted more of Remi and he was close to saying 'fuck this' and just going to him.

Time slowly ticked by. Yeah, he was watching the clock. At eleven-thirty, he left the house. He was going to be early, but he had to get out of there. If he could have afforded it, he would have spent the week in a hotel. As much as he loved his home, right now it hurt to be there.

The restaurant wasn't far from his house. They were going to a new pho place he'd heard good things about. Sara Jo had beaten him there and it was good to see her. He'd missed her but he was very happy she'd moved up. It was everything she deserved.

"Hey, you're here early." El walked toward her.

She stood up and gave him a hug.

"I knew you'd leave your house too soon and I wanted to get here before you did."

They both sat down.

"God, it's good to see you, Sara Jo. I've missed you at work."

"I've been so busy that I haven't had time to think about anything but the new job this week. I'm sorry I haven't been there."

"It's okay. You don't need to be around me right now. It's a happy time for you and I'm just sad all the time. Well, when I'm not angry."

Sara Jo put her hand on his. "I'm still here for you. If you're having a hard time, call me."

"I know. I wanted to let you settle in before I dropped all my problems on you."

"That's now how it works, Elros. You're sad? You call. End of story. That's what friends are for. You know — happiness and sadness, health and wealth, that kind of stuff."

"Um-m, I think that's what spouses are for. Those are wedding vows." El chuckled.

He was so happy to see Sara Jo. She could make him laugh like no other.

She shrugged. "Maybe, but, you know it's true. I've known you for a long time. You like to keep everything bottled up. You don't share. It isn't good for you."

Their waiter showed up, so he didn't have a chance to respond. They ordered. He got a banh mi and Sara Jo ordered a pho with everything in it. He couldn't wait to try the food. He was actually hungry for a change

"Back to what I was saying. You hold stuff in. Have you talked to Remi?"

"No. Well, not since I went to his dad's place. I told him I needed time. I saw him at work on Monday, but that was it."

"I haven't talked to him either. I'm worried."

"I'm sure he's fine."

"Maybe, but I'm going to his apartment tomorrow if I can't get a hold of him. Kiki has been fielding his calls — from *me*. It isn't like him. And you need to stop this nonsense that you can't be with him because you're a mess. Let him be there for you."

"I can't. Not yet. I want to get through Mom's stuff and figure out the bills."

"That could take forever."

"Yes, it could, but— I might have to sell the house."

"No!"

"Yes. The market is good right now. It's located in a great spot. I'm sure it would sell with no problem."

"You love that place, El. You can't sell."

"Sometimes you have to do things you don't want to. It's called being an adult."

"Being an adult sucks. There has to be another way. I'll help you find it. Hell, Remi would too."

"And that's why I'm *not* going to him right now. He would help me. I know he would, but I don't want him for his money, Sara Jo. Living in an apartment won't be so bad."

"Don't rush into anything yet. Okay?"

"I want it behind me. I want to have happy memories of my mom and not break down so much. If selling the house helps with it, I'm all for it."

"If you rush into something like this while you're still emotional, you might regret it. I don't want you to sell the place and months later come to realize that you did the wrong thing."

"That's why you're a friend. I won't rush it, but if it has to happen, I'm going forward with it."

"Deal."

The soup and sandwich arrived at the table. El dug into his lunch. He couldn't believe how hungry he was.

"You haven't been eating, have you?" Sara Jo raised an eyebrow.

El shook his head. "I haven't been hungry."

"Well, this is a good sign."

He shrugged. "I guess. I am happy to get out of the house. I've been going through so many things and feel stuck there sometimes. This is much better." El raised his sandwich and wiggled it at Sara Jo before taking another bite.

"I can help."

"I know you can, but…let's talk about something else. How is the job going?"

"Why did I let you talk me into doing this? I was perfectly happy to be Remi's admin. I liked the job, and I enjoy the company."

"You're still with the company."

"I know, but this is different. I'm in charge."

"You love to be in charge, Sara Jo. It's the bossy side of you."

"Whatever." Sara Jo waved a hand at El.

"It's true. You try that crap on me all the time."

"But you never listen."

"I listen sometimes." El shrugged.

"Not enough. But, you aren't wrong. I do enjoy being the boss. It's a big learning curve for me. At least the employees aren't giving me grief. They've been really helpful. I understand some of the business because we've use steel companies all the time for our projects. I know we have a system in place at the fab shop for when we do work for the construction division of the company. I'm setting up something similar for us for billing purposes, to keep everything on the level. It isn't like we'll just be supplying for Marlow. There is a customer list. It's exciting to be on this end of things, but stressful."

"And you're loving every minute of it."

"Of course I am." Sara Jo laughed.

"I'm happy for you."

"It wouldn't have happened if you hadn't suggested it to Remi. He's a great guy."

El sighed. "Yes, he is. I miss him."

"You don't have to. Talk to him."

"Not yet. I told him I needed time and I meant it."

"We're back to that. You're allowed to show him you're hurting."

"It isn't just that."

"Really?" Sara Jo glared at him.

"Really. We just talked about this. Let's go back to talking about your job."

"How about we finish up and head to your place? I'll help you with your mom's stuff. It'll get done faster that way."

"I'll take you up on that. I want to get it over with. I plan to donate what I can."

"That's great."

"Once I get through her bedroom, there are things in the attic that I need to pull down and go through. I might as cull out my stuff too and do a full cleansing. And, if I have to sell the place, at least I'll have a head start on emptying the place."

"Stop."

"I'm being realistic."

"You love that place."

"I do. But it might be for the best. It hurts to be there without her." El put his sandwich down. His appetite was disappearing.

"Oh, honey, I know."

El watched Sara Jo finish her soup. The ups and downs of grief were too much. One minute he was fine, then he was crying and the anger would hit after. Would it ever go away? It had to.

"Thanks for being here. I love you."

"I love you too. Let's get the check and get out of here."

* * * *

As soon as he stepped into his mom's room, he wanted to leave. It smelled like her favorite perfume. El put his hand over his mouth to suppress his sob. Sara Jo wrapped her arms around his waist and hugged him.

"I can go through it for you." She squeezed him before letting go.

"No. No. I can do this. I have to. It'll be cathartic." El took a deep breath and went to his mom's closet. "Most of her clothes can be donated." He grabbed a box and started throwing clothes into it.

"If that's the case, I'll start with her dresser. Hand me a box."

They worked in silence through the afternoon, sorting and packing. It didn't take them as long as he'd thought it would. His mom didn't have a lot of things.

"I think I'm done for now."

"Okay, if you're sure. I can come back tomorrow." Sara Jo closed up the box she'd been working on. "Why don't we load this up into my car? I know a shelter that I can give them to."

"That's a great idea. Thank you. I'm going to have to find a place to donate her dresser. I gave the bed away when we rented the hospital one.

"There's a new women's shelter that's just starting up. They could use it, I'm sure. That's where I was going to take the clothes," Sara Jo said.

"If you could let them know about the dresser, I can drop it off. Or, if they want to come here with a truck, I have a few more things they can have."

"I'll call them tomorrow. It's getting late."

"How about I order us a pizza? Are you getting hungry?"

"I could always eat some pizza."

"Good. I'll call for it before I take the boxes out to your car. Tomorrow I might start on the living room. Most of the stuff in there is hers."

"Are you keeping anything?"

"Maybe a couple of things, like some of her books. She has a copy of *Gone with the Wind* that I got her. It's from the 1930s. It's was from the second run, and it doesn't have a cover, so it isn't worth anything. Well, to me it is."

"It'll get easier. It won't go away, but it *will* get easier."

El turned so he could hug Sara Jo. "In my head I know I that. It's my heart that won't catch up."

He rested his chin on her head and held her close. Her stomach grumbled.

"Dude, I love you, but order that pizza." She laughed.

"Got it."

If it weren't for packing up clothes, it would have been a nice afternoon in with a friend. He needed this bit of normal. Maybe things would get better.

Chapter Twenty-Seven

Knock, knock, knock.

Remi groaned. *What is that noise?*

His head hurt, and he didn't know what was going on.

Knock, knock, knock.

It happened again. He was blind. Everything was dark. He struggled against something on top of him.

Where the hell am I?

He finally got the blanket off and opened his eyes. He wasn't blind, but his head hurt. The pounding was intense.

Knock, knock, knock.

"I know you're in there. Open the door."

It wasn't in his head. He was at his apartment. In his bed. Someone was at his door.

Remi shuffled out of the room, the blanket wrapped around him like a cape. He threw open the door, turned around and went to his couch.

"Are you sick?" Sara Jo sat beside him.

He shook his head. It was going to fall off his head. He grabbed it between his hands.

"Dying," he croaked out.

"Are you *drunk*?" Sara Jo sniffed at him.

Remi tilted over and half-lay on the couch.

"What is it with the two of you and alcohol?"

"Who? What?"

"Nothing. You haven't been to work in days. How do I know that? I had to grill Kiki. She was covering for you. So, good call moving her up. You have stuff to get done."

Remi sat up. "What day is it?" He squinted. It was so bright in the living room. He should go back to his bedroom and hibernate again.

"It's Tuesday. Don't make me call your father."

"Are you sure it isn't Sunday?"

"Um—pretty sure since... You know... *I* went to work on Monday and today."

"Fuck." He lay back down and put the cover over his head. "Wait... I went to work Monday."

"What is *wrong* with you?"

"I'm screwed. And how did you get up here?"

"No, you aren't. And some guy was coming in. I just followed him." Sara Jo shrugged.

"Work isn't everything."

"It isn't. When did *you* figure that out? You've always been a workaholic."

"Elros." He whispered the name. Like if he said it out loud, it would get away from him.

"Oh, Remi. He's hurting too."

"I know. And I can't— He won't let— I just want to be there for him. God, my head hurts."

"Well, you've lost a few days, because the Monday you went to work was last week."

"That can't be right."

"It is. I have no idea what you've been doing, but you haven't been in the office."

"I did the staff meeting and —"

"El told me about it. We went to lunch this weekend and I helped him get some stuff together for charity. He might have to sell the house."

"But…he can't."

"I told him that too, but he has bills that are more than he can take care of."

"I'll do it." Remi stood up and threw his blanket off.

"Dude!"

"What?" Remi glanced around.

"You should probably put some clothes on." Sara Jo had her hands over her eyes.

He looked down to see that he was only in a pair of boxer briefs. Remi picked the blanket back up and wrapped it around himself.

"Sorry." Remi began to pace. It hurt, but he didn't care.

"It's not like you can do anything right now, Remi. But you need to get yourself together."

"I can pay all the medical bills, so he doesn't have to. He can't lose that house." Remi ran a hand through his hair.

"Remi, that's one of the reasons he wants space. He needs to figure this out on his own. He doesn't want to use you."

"But I want to. I have the money. It's something I can do."

"You don't think he knows that, Remi? He could so easily run to you and ask you to fix it, but he wants to come to you strong."

"He is the strongest person I know, Sara Jo. To go through what he did with his mom while working the whole time? I admire him so much. If I can't be there for him in person, I need to do…something." Remi waved his hands around and lost his blanket again. He moved to pick it back up. He really should get dressed, but this was too important.

"Let him come to you." Sara Jo stood in front of him. He almost ran over her but stopped.

"I'm doing this, Sara Jo. If I don't do anything else for him, I am *not* letting him lose his childhood home. It means everything to him. He already lost his mom. He needs that house."

"I didn't tell you all this, so you could run in and play white knight, but I have to say, I'm sort of happy you are going to help him. You should know, though, that he won't be happy."

"I miss him."

Sara Jo wrapped her arms around Remi. "He misses you too. He might not say it, but I can see it. He wants to be whole for you and thinks he needs to get over his grief first and take care of his bills. If you interfere, it might hurt your relationship."

"Right now, we don't have a relationship. He won't let me be there for him and I don't want to push him. I really don't—but this I can do."

"What if he decides he wants to get rid of the house?"

"He should be able to figure that out without the thread of *having* to get rid of it because of medical bills."

"I agree with you, but maybe you should talk to him first." Sara Jo rubbed her hands up and down Remi's arms.

"I need your help. You should get me the information I need to pay the bills. I can do that, right? It isn't like I want the information. I just want to give them money."

"You aren't going to talk to him, are you?"

"No."

"He's going to find out."

"Maybe he'll come talk to me when he does." Remi went back to the couch. His head was really starting to pound again.

"I'll find out what I can, but I still think you should speak with him first. Now, get yourself together and get into work."

"What time is it?"

"It's almost one. I came here on my lunch hour because I couldn't get a hold of you."

"This isn't like me." Remi sighed.

"It really isn't. I don't know if you've ever missed a day. Heck, you've even come in sick."

"It took this moment in my life to realize that work isn't everything, that I need to get out of my shell and open up my heart. I think El and I have something. We were just starting when Harry fucked things up. If it wasn't for him, I would be there with El right now, helping him through one of the worst things in his life. But, instead, I'm here, wallowing in my self-pity and drinking myself stupid. I didn't know it would hurt this bad. I really didn't."

"No more drinking." Sara Jo shook a finger at him.

"I make no promises."

"Remi…"

"Sara Jo…"

"You have responsibilities. You can't drop everything to become a raging alcoholic."

"I won't." Remi rubbed a hand over his chest. "You're right. I do need to get back to work, but—I am going to start delegating more. I have perfectly good managers. They're going to have to step up. I'm not living for work anymore."

"You can't switch one obsession for another."

"I'm not, but if I can get El to see me again, I want to do this right, and that means not working twenty hours a day. I want to take him places and also spend some time with my dad. If I've learned anything, it's that you can lose someone so fast. There is no going back from that. I don't want to feel like I'm missing something because I'm so focused on work, when I don't have to be. Not that I'm planning on giving it up, though. But now that there are three companies under our belt and with Dad getting ready to retire, it's up to me to keep them running. I have you in charge of the mill. We're going to find someone to take over for Dad and I'm going to do the same for the fabrication division. I'll have my projects, but I'm not going to be as hands on, not anymore. It's time to step back."

"Listen to you, going all adult on me. I don't know what to say."

"You don't have to say anything, but I need to thank you for being there for me all these years."

"You are not going to make me cry, Remington Marlow!" Sara Jo wiped a finger under her eye.

"It's the truth. And now you're doing even more. I know I don't have to worry with you in charge. You could do something for me."

"What's that?"

"Help me figure out who should head up the fabrication division."

"You've got it. Now, you need to get in the shower and go to work. You don't have a head of the division yet, so you have work to do. You've got two new projects going on, plus, I heard you're planning to quote some stuff for the new riverfront project."

"I did that to get out of the office."

"It was a smart break, but that's why you're the boss."

"You know, I miss you too."

"Kiki is coming along. You won't miss me for long. Plus, I'm El's best friend and I still work for you. I'm not going anywhere."

"Good. I hope you know that I'm your friend too."

"I know that. If I didn't, I wouldn't be here right now trying to get your ass back into the office. Now stop feeling sorry for yourself. Even if El doesn't come back to you, you have to live your life."

"You're right. I know it. I even told him when we started with the fake dating that I wouldn't hold it against him if he didn't say yes. I don't intend to hold it against him now that he needs time. He's good at his job. I don't want him to leave the company because of me. It's one of the reasons I'm not pushing. He needs that job."

"He could get one somewhere else," Sara Jo suggested.

"We're the best in town."

"Ego much?" Sara Jo grinned.

"It isn't ego when it's true. Marlow, Inc. is all about the employees."

"You are. Now, get out there and get that business so the employees can reap the rewards. I'm going back to work because I need to finish setting up the intercompany billing process and I have to hire a new assistant."

"What? Why?"

"The guy who had the job didn't like working for a woman, so he quit."

"That's— Why didn't I know someone was in that company who thought that way?"

"It wasn't like he was going to tell the big boss. It's fine. It'll be nice to find someone who I can work with."

"If you need anything, let me know. I'll do better about answering my phone. Promise."

"Good. And I'll be here to kick your ass if you need it."

"Thank you."

Sara Jo stood up and Remi followed her lead. He pulled her into his arms for another hug. He was lucky to have someone like her in his life. He had a lot to be grateful for and he needed to remember that in the future. It didn't matter if El decided to let him into his personal life or not. Remi still had a lot to be thankful for.

"Don't make me come back here, Remi."

He walked her to the door. "I won't."

"Good. I'll get back to you with a list of people who could take over the day-to-day of the fabrication division and, against my better judgment, I'll get you the information you need to pay El's mom's medical bills."

Remi nodded and let her out of the apartment. He had a job to do and a shower to take. It was time to stop the pity party.

Chapter Twenty-Eight

"Mr. Marlow, what are you doing here?" El opened the door and stood back to let him into the house.

It was after six and he'd just settled in to do…nothing. He had been thinking about dinner, but the knock on the door had interrupted him. It was probably for the best, as he'd started to think about his mom and that would have brought him back to being a blubbering mess.

"I wanted to see how you're doing. Remi told me about your mother. I'm so sorry. I don't think I told you that when you were at the ranch the other day." Mr. Marlow held out his hand so El could shake it.

"You didn't have to stop by for that, Mr. Marlow."

"I thought I told you to call me Jackson." Jackson gave him a small grin.

"Yes, sir. Um…Jackson. Can I get you anything to drink?" El led Jackson to the living room and gestured toward the couch so he could sit down.

"No. I'm fine. I just wanted to see how you were doing. Remi told me about the whole fake boyfriend thing."

That was like ripping the Band-Aid off. El had never planned for Jackson to find out. He knew Remi didn't want him to know.

"Oh no. I'm sorry. He shouldn't have to— I mean I should have—" El paced around the room, his hands in his pockets.

Remi's dad shouldn't have found out, and it was probably his fault for not keeping up appearances. He didn't want to bring a rift between father and son. He was a bad fake boyfriend.

"I knew all along. I was hoping the two of you would hit it off." Jackson sat down on the couch.

The place was messy, but it couldn't be helped with all the packing he was doing. He'd come to terms with the fact that it was for the best to sell the house.

"We did." Did he sound wistful?

God, had they hit it off. If he wasn't being so stubborn, he could be with Remi now. He knew it, but he wasn't ready. Not yet. Once the sale went through and he got back on steady ground, he'd go to Remi and ask him out.

"Then why is my son so miserable?"

"I—I need some time." El shrugged. It was the truth.

"Not because of that Harry nonsense, I hope." Jackson waved a hand in the air, like he was dismissing the idea.

"At first, yes, but it didn't take long for me to realize that it couldn't be what it looked like. I've talked to Sara Jo some about it. It hurt. I won't lie. And I shouldn't be talking to you about this."

"I'm happy you're humoring an old man. So, what seems to be the problem?"

"I think that should be between me and Remi." El stopped in front of Jackson.

"It should. I totally agree. Normally I wouldn't stick my nose so deeply into something not my business. But the thing is, when I had dinner with you and Remi at his apartment, I could see the connection and now? All I see is hurt. I want him to be happy. He's my only son and I don't want him to be a lonely old man."

"There are things I'm dealing with." El didn't say any more. It sounded stupid when he said it out loud.

"I know. Believe me, I know. When my wife died, I almost went with her. If it hadn't been for Remi, I would have. I loved that woman something fierce."

"I'm sorry."

"It was a while ago. It still hurts. That's the thing with loss. It never really goes away, and you just learn to deal with it better."

"It's more than that. I need to figure out where I stand and I want to be whole before I talk to Remi."

"He doesn't need you whole, son. He just needs you."

"Thank you for coming here. I really do appreciate it."

"I can take a hint. I really shouldn't have come over, and I'm sure Remi will yell at me. I have never seen my son as happy as he was when the two of you were faking it. I want more of that for him. For too long he has used his work as an excuse. I don't want that for him anymore. Oh, by the way, a little bird told me he plans on paying off your bills so you don't have to sell the house." Jackson got up and walked out of the house.

El was too stunned to move. It was happening, the one thing he didn't want. He needed to stand on even ground with Remi. Sure, he'd never have the money Remi did, but he wanted to be able to take care of himself.

He couldn't let that happen. He wasn't going to be some kept man. Remi hadn't been at work the last few days. At least, El didn't think he had been. There had been no sign of him after that staff meeting the past Monday, but it wasn't unusual for El to not see him in the office.

El decided that he was going over to that apartment and they were going to have it out. He had come to terms with selling the house. It's what his mom would have wanted. There was no way she'd want him to be stuck in the place where she'd died. Too many memories would keep him stuck in the past. It was time, and he was fine with it.

Paying off the medical bills was something he could do as well. He wanted a relationship with Remi. He did, and to others it might not look that way, but he had fallen...hard. And if Remi paid off his medical bills, where would that leave El? In debt to the man—and that was what he'd been trying to avoid. El didn't want the money to come between them.

He grabbed his phone and keys. He was going to talk to Mr. Remington Marlow and give him a piece of his mind. How dare he take control of El's life that way? He wasn't after Remi for his money and he was going to make that clear while he yelled at him.

He left the house and jumped into his car. He was a man on a mission, and that mission was to make Remi back off.

Traffic was horrible. Everyone in Fort Wayne had to be going out to dinner. Road construction didn't help, as some roads were down to one lane. He hated road construction season but he finally made it. He parked in the garage a few blocks down and walked toward the apartment. It helped cool him down some, but he was still going to give Remi a piece of his mind. It was his life and El needed to deal with it in his own way. Remi would have to understand that.

El was lucky that someone was coming out of the apartment complex as he was going in so he didn't have to be buzzed up by Remi. A sneak attack was the best way to go. He hoped Remi was home. He needed to clear the air. It was past time. He should have talked to him last week. He knew now that it was pride stopping him.

He knocked on the door. No one answered so he knocked again.

"Hold on." Remi flung open the door. "Elros," he whispered.

El didn't get a chance to say anything. Remi pulled him through the door and hugged him tight. El closed his eyes, sighed and relaxed into Remi. It was like coming home.

"I didn't think I'd ever be able to do this again." Remi nuzzled El's neck.

"Remi..."

He didn't say anything else. He wasn't able to. Remi kissed him. El lost himself in the sensation. He needed this, like he never knew he did. He started to cry.

"No, El. Please don't cry." Remi wiped his tears with his thumb. "Come in. Sit down."

El nodded. He wasn't angry anymore, but he still needed to talk to Remi.

"I missed you." That wasn't what he'd intended to say. It seemed his mouth had a mind of its own and it was listening to his heart, not his head.

"I missed you too, but I didn't want to push."

"That's not what your dad said…" El sat back on the couch and crossed his arms.

It needed to be said and he wouldn't be distracted by Remi, even if the hand on his thigh made his body tingle.

"My dad?"

"He came over to my house."

"What? He shouldn't have done that. I'm so sorry. Wait! Did I read this wrong? Are you here to tell me you never want to see me again? Oh, please God, don't let it be that." Remi turned and grabbed El's hands in his.

"I have a very important question to ask you, Remi. I need you to be honest with me. Okay?"

Remi nodded.

"Good. Okay—are you planning on paying off my bills?"

"Well—" Remi bit his bottom lip. "Yes." He sighed.

El stood up. "You can't do that!"

Remi stood up as well and faced off with El.

"I have to. Don't you see? You've lost so much. You can't let the house go too."

"That's my decision, Remi. You didn't even ask me. One of the reasons I needed time was because I had to figure out what my plans were. I didn't want to burden you with my problems. I have to do it on my own. I can't rely on your money to fix things."

"But, El, I have the money. I have more money than I can possibly spend in one lifetime. I want to help you and it's something I can do."

"No."

"But—"

"*No.* I am *not* here for your money. I have *never* been here for your money. If we're going to do this, you can't just buy me everything. I won't be a kept man. I need to contribute. And you taking over by paying my bills behind my back isn't going to let me trust you."

"The house— Wait! Did you say 'if'?"

"I did. I should have talked to you before this, but I was being stubborn. I want to work on us. I want us to date. But I don't want you taking care of everything. As for the house, it's just a place."

"You grew up there. You have all these memories."

"Mom wouldn't have wanted me to stay there. She told me before she died that the one thing she regretted was not traveling. So, I know she wouldn't want me stuck with the house or with the bills. I've thought about it and it's time."

"Then move in here."

El went to Remi and took him in his arms. "Not yet. We can talk about it, but for now, I'm going to find a place of my own. We're too new. I want to get to know you better. I want to go on dates."

"Are you sure?"

"I'm sure. If you want to help, you can clean the house with me and get it ready for sale. It's paid in full, so the money from it should pay off what bills I have and if it doesn't, I'm sure I can get on some sort of payment plan. I've got this. Let me come to you with both my feet on the ground. I want us to be equal and I want to pull my weight in this relationship."

"You said 'relationship'." Remi grinned before picking him up and spinning him around the room.

El laughed. It was nice to be happy. He'd been so sad and he didn't need to carry the pain by himself. Remi would be there for him with all the hugs and kisses he'd need. That's what made relationships so great, and he was ready to start this one in the right way. There would be nothing fake about it.

Epilogue

Three years later

"I can't believe we're doing this. Are you sure?" Remi reached for El's hand and squeezed.

"It's too late now." El turned to grin at his husband.

Husband. Three years before, El never would have thought he'd say those words, but here he was with the man he loved. Two years before, they'd moved in together. They'd kept Remi's apartment for a while, but eventually they'd needed more space — something with a fenced-in backyard.

"I know. She'll be here any minute." Rem paced the waiting room.

"These things take time." El stepped in front of Remi to stop his movement around the room.

"We should be in there."

"She wants to do it by herself. You know that. It was in the agreement."

"I know. I know." Remi put his forehead against El's.

"Did I miss it?" Jackson raced into the room. He had a big teddy bear in his arms.

Remi turned toward his father. El was still smiling.

"No, Dad. She's still in labor."

"Why aren't you in there?" Jackson put the bear on one of the chairs.

"She wanted to do this part on her own. We told you that. As soon as she is almost there, we'll go in. She's been a surrogate before, so she's an old hat at this." Remi hugged Jackson. "It's why we chose her in the first place."

"Mr. Carter-Marlow."

"Yes," El and Remi said at the same time.

"It's time. She's ready to push." The nurse turned and went back to the room.

El just stood there. It was really happening, and he couldn't believe it.

"Boys, go!" Jackson pushed them toward the room.

El didn't need to be told twice. Well maybe he did, but he grabbed Remi's hand and pulled him. Their baby was coming, and they were going to be there to see it happen. He never thought he'd be a father. His mom would be so happy. It was just too bad that she hadn't lived long enough to meet her granddaughter.

They'd finally closed on the house the previous week and were doing the baby's room in all pink. Remi had tried to tell him it was too much, but El didn't care. He was bringing their princess home to pink—and frills. Remi asked what he'd do if their daughter was a tomboy. El had told him that they'd change the room, but for now…pink.

Remi peeked around the door and El followed him. Their surrogate was there with her husband. El was still in shock that the couple had agreed to carry their baby.

In two years, if they wanted another child, she had agreed to one more time. This time, they'd used El's sperm. The next time they'd use Remi's. They were going to be a big happy family and Jackson was over the moon at having grandkids.

"How's it going?" Remi whispered.

"She's good, a natural at having babies." Rick wiped Jill's forehead and looked at her with so much love.

It was how Remi looked at him every day. The love Remi showed him was enough to fill two hearts, but he was all El's. Jill sat up a little, her face going dark red.

"That's it, push. We're almost there." The doctor between Jill's legs encouraged her. "We've got a full head of hair here, Daddies."

The doctor was Jill's and knew all about the situation, which made it easier. It was all in her birth plan. They'd talked about what would go on, but it was so surreal to be there in the room and watch *his* baby being born. Remi was going to make such a wonderful dad.

"One more big push, Jill."

She grunted and strained, her husband at her side, rubbing her back and whispering in her ear. There was some classical music playing in the background, but soon the only sound echoing around the room was their baby girl.

The doctor handed the baby off to the nurse, who cleaned her up and weighed and measured her. Then she gestured for him and Remi to follow her.

"Thank you. Both of you." Remi had tears in his eyes and a smile on his lips.

Rick nodded to them before giving his wife his full attention. Rick had lost his brother to a gay-bashing and it was one of the reasons the two of them had agreed for Jill to be a surrogate to gay couples. Well…two gay couples. Jill had let them know that after she had their second child, she was done. El didn't blame her. It couldn't be good for her body.

El followed Remi and the nurse to another room.

"Who would like to hold her first?"

He led Remi to the chair and made him sit down. "You hold her first. I'm going to get your dad." El squeezed Remi's shoulder.

It was so overwhelming.

"What's her name?" he heard the nurse ask.

"Kathleen Jo," was Remi's reply.

"A pretty name for a pretty girl."

El teared up. It hit him in the heart. It hurt, but in a good way. They had agreed to name their daughter after his mom and their best friend. God, he wished his mom could have been there.

"Jackson…"

"Is she here?"

"She is. Come on." El led Remi's dad back to the room.

Remi had his shirt open and Kathy Jo was skin-to-skin with him. They'd read up on what to do with a newborn. They'd done so much research to make sure they were doing everything right.

"She's so tiny." Remi kissed her head.

"You look like a natural." El moved closer and looked down at their baby girl.

She had a full head of hair and she was small. But she had all her fingers and toes. El counted, just to be sure.

"Wash your hands then switch spots with me." Remi stood and moved out of the rocker.

El was hesitant because he didn't want to break her, but he quickly washed up and sat down. He held out his arms.

"Just remember to cradle her head." Remi eased her into his arms.

"Hello, Kathy Jo. Welcome to the world."

"Kathy Jo. I love it." Remi ran a finger over Kathy's cheek.

It was love at first sight. El didn't know his heart could be so full. "You are going to be so loved," he assured her.

"And spoiled. Grandpa wants a turn." Jackson washed his hands and waited for El to move out of the chair.

El went to stand beside Remi and they watched his dad whisper to the baby.

"I should text Sara Jo. She's going to want to see her goddaughter," El said.

"It's okay, El. I just did. She's on her way. She yelled at me for not calling earlier," Remi replied, grinning.

"I bet she did. Did you tell her the baby's name?" They had been keeping it to themselves until after she was born.

"I didn't. I figured we could tell her together when she gets here."

El laid his head on Remi's shoulder. He was at peace. It still hurt when he thought of his mom, but he didn't grieve as hard as he had that first month. Remi had been so strong, standing beside him and holding him when he'd needed it.

He loved his husband more than anyone in the world, except for Kathy. She had his heart from the first cry.

"Can you believe we're daddies, Remi?"

"No. It doesn't seem real yet, even after holding her. I keep waiting for someone to come in and say 'Psych! No baby for you'." Remi kissed El's forehead.

"I can't wait to take her home." El hugged Remi close.

"The nurse said that if everything goes all right, we can take her home tomorrow."

"I'm nervous," El admitted.

"Me too," Remi responded, "but Dad said he'd stay over the first few days. He has plenty of experience. Granted, it has been years, but he's one up on us."

"You boys have made me so happy." Jackson looked away from Kathy for a moment to beam at them. "I'm going to be the best grandpa ever."

"Yes, you are." Remi agreed.

"I heard there was a baby around here who needs her Auntie Sara Jo." The door opened to the room and in came their best friend. El was so happy to see her. If it hadn't been for her and Jackson, he wouldn't be where he was right now, because he would have given Remi up for pride's sake.

"Kathleen Jo is ready to meet you," El announced.

"Jo? Kathleen *Jo*? El! I'm going to cry." She through her arms around El, then Remi.

"Go wash your hands so you can hold her." Remi tilted his head toward the sink.

Jackson reluctantly relinquished the baby. The nurse came in shortly after Sara Jo had sat down.

"Hello, Dads. I'm going to need to do the hearing test. I brought the equipment in, but I'm going to need the bundle of joy. She's going to need her first bottle and might need a diaper change too."

After the testing was complete, the flow of the hospital settled down. Kathy rested while El watched her breathe. Remi had fallen asleep on the bed a few minutes before, but El couldn't sleep.

"Your grandma would have loved you. I can't wait to tell you all about her. We're going to be the best dads in the world, and you're going to want for nothing. You have a lot of love on your side. We'll share it all with you. And…I might even talk your dad into a puppy."

"Promising her the moon already?" Remi put his arms around him.

"I thought you were asleep."

"I was, but I heard you talking."

"I'm sorry. I didn't mean to wake you up."

"It's okay. This moment with you is one of the best of my life. And I figure, this is the quiet before the storm. Soon we'll be at home and there won't be a nurse to call if we have questions."

"Well, to answer your earlier question, yes. I'm offering her the moon, just like you did with me. I love you, Remington Carter-Marlow."

"I love you too, Elros Carter-Marlow."

The world was a beautiful place when El was in love and had the world at his feet. Tomorrow would be another day, and it would be glorious, as he started his next adventure with his husband and daughter. He was so happy that he'd taken the billionaire's bribe. It had been the start of the rest of his life—and El couldn't be happier.

Want to see more from this author? Here's a taster for you to enjoy!

Vegas Sin
Jambrea Jo Jones

Excerpt

Owen Carpenter strolled through the precinct like he hadn't a care in the world. He whistled some song that was on the radio before he shut the car off. Now it would be stuck in his head all day. He might as well share it with others. What could he say, he was a giver.

It helped the façade he put on for others and it drove his partner nuts when he did it, which was a plus. He always had the outward appearance of being calm and that everything was right in the world. He had to or he'd go batshit crazy and he couldn't have that. He was armed, after all, and it could be dangerous for a cop to go all mental. He needed to be focused, and if pushing his issues back helped, he'd do it all day. Owen tried to keep his private and work lives separate. That didn't always happen, because his partner liked to give him a hard time, which was why Owen did his best to drive Jeff crazy. Of course they were more like brothers than partners. Most days that was a good thing, especially when Jeff's wife sent in muffins for him. The best was when Sally came in and personally handed him some goody to make sure Owen got some. Jeff hated that and tried to steal his goodies, but Sally made sure Owen was taken care of.

This morning was one for the books, that was for sure. One of those days he wished he could do over. His sister and niece had been kicked out of their latest apartment the night before, so they were shacked up with him for the duration. He had to haul all their stuff to his place, and it was a mess. At least he had a garage to hold some of the stuff. Not that his sister was kicked out of her home every day, but Susan wasn't the best with her money on a good day. He tried to help the best he could, but she didn't always appreciate her big brother butting his nose into her business. At least Susan hadn't gone back to the booze. That would add a whole other set of issues he really didn't want to deal with. He'd helped get her dry once and hoped like hell it stuck because he didn't know if he could go through that again.

His niece, Gabbi, was a sweetheart, and he'd do anything for her. She was only nine and cute as a button with her long blonde hair and big blue eyes. Yeah, he might be wrapped around her little finger, but he didn't know if he'd ever do kids, so she might be all he ever had. He planned to spoil her as much as possible. When the time came, he'd make sure she was treated right by whoever she wanted to date. If he let her date. She was an old soul who acted more like Susan's mom on most occasions, which made him want to pamper Gabbi even more.

His own mom had trouble dealing with two new people in her space — when she remembered it was her space. The Alzheimer's was getting worse. It was hard enough most days when she didn't remember him, but now she kept asking who the two hussies were and why they were in her house. Gabbi didn't fully understand why her grandma couldn't remember her and called her names.

His mom was in the process of being moved to a new home this week because taking care of her was just too much. He hated the fact that she had to go, but it was past time. A nurse came by to sit with her while he worked. The only problem with that was that they didn't always send the same person and it got confusing for his mom. If she was in a home, she could get used to the same people. It would give her a bit of the stability she'd lost the last few years. At least with his sister at the house, he could get some help with their mom — not that Mother would remember either of them — but Susan needed to help out. Breakfast had been a disaster with his mom dumping her food on the floor and stomping out of the room like a cranky two year old. Poor Gabbi had had to do some clean up, because Susan had decided to sleep in, and he'd been running late for work. He made a note to take Gabbi to a movie or shopping for the weekend. If she really wanted to go, he'd take her, even if he hated going to the mall.

Now he needed coffee — stat. He hated the slop they had in the office, but it was better than nothing. He'd forgotten to set his coffeemaker up to brew last night. Of course, he'd been dealing with a sobbing sister and a too-serious niece. He hoped that nothing big had been tossed on his desk, but he wasn't sure he'd get that lucky. It had been a busy week — not that he should be surprised — since it was Vegas, after all. The lights and gambling attracted all kinds. It kept him busy most days. Owen had just wrapped up a case late yesterday. A domestic violence situation where the boyfriend had killed the girlfriend. It was pretty open and shut, but he'd still had to cross his T's and dot his I's so the guy didn't get off on a technicality.

At least he wasn't set to testify anytime soon. He hated going to court. He'd rather be solving cases. Some of the other guys looked at it like a day off, but not him. All those people staring at him while he did his best not to fidget in the seat.

His partner was out on leave so that left him picking up the slack. They had a few cases open that he'd have to take a look at and see what else he could do, as long as something new didn't take priority.

The coffeepot was almost empty. There probably wasn't even enough for a cup. It seemed the guys did that shit all the time. Owen poured the little bit into his cup. At least it would give him a jolt while he waited for a fresh batch to brew. He didn't even think about how long the pot had been setting there. The others would pass it up in a heartbeat and wait until someone else made it, then they would all jump on it like vultures. Shit. He really should have brewed some at home.

Maybe he would swing by a Starbucks later. He hated to spend the extra money, but he couldn't live without the nectar of the gods. The sludge in his cup wasn't going to cut it. After one sip, he dumped it out. Nothing was going to save that coffee. Leaving the pot brewing, he made his way to his desk. It was pretty quiet. The shift change meeting wouldn't happen for about an hour, so he had time to go through the files from yesterday.

Owen had just settled in when his captain threw a file on his desk. He knew he wouldn't be lucky enough to skate through the day with the files he already had. He'd jinxed himself.

"Kidnapping. This is the fifth one in as many weeks. They're all tall, blonde, mid- to late twenties. That's about the only thing they have in common. One is a local and the other four were all staying at different hotels. I want you and Polubinsky on this."

"He's on leave." Owen picked up the file.

"You can start on it. He'll catch up. Take a look at the notes and do some legwork. This one takes top priority for now. I want them found. None of them have shown up dead yet, and I'd like to keep it that way. There have been no demands or ransom calls. The first couple were filed and looked at briefly, but nothing came of it. When the third was reported, we noted a pattern. Now that we have five, we have to consider that they might be connected. None of the vics look like the types who would just walk off, but you never can tell. You know how it is. Most of them can be chalked up to having too much fun, but it's been weeks on the first two girls. The local lady has a kid and appears responsible. She has lived here in Vegas her whole life, so I don't see her running off now." The captain shrugged and left.

Owen flipped through the file. There wasn't much there, just a description of each girl and where they were from, the hotels where they had stayed. They were all over the place. One of the hotels caught his eye — Totally Five Star. He'd take a look at that one last. He had a friend who dealt cards there. Plus it was the place he loved to go once a month. He'd missed last month and it looked like he was going to miss this month too with all the stuff going on.

At least now he could get that cup of coffee he wanted. Plus he'd get out of the morning meetings, which could get boring, especially if Espinoza got to talking. It sucked that it had to take a foul-play case to get him out into the streets, but he'd take it.

It was only eight in the morning and it was already reaching the hundreds. One of the things he loved and hated about Vegas, but it was his city, so he dealt with it. He really couldn't imagine living anywhere else.

First stop for interviews would be to the local girl's family. It looked like she was the first one taken. He just hoped the leads hadn't run dry with that one. It sucked that sometimes it took a murder to find these people. Most of the time they turned up safe and sound. For some they just needed time away from the world. Hell, he could understand that. At times he wished he could run away, but he had too much responsibility and he wouldn't leave like that. It just wasn't in him to flee his duties.

Who would take care of his mom or his sister, not to mention Gabbi? If anyone needed him, it was the kid. He was the only one she could act her own age with.

PUBLISHING

Sign up for our newsletter and find out about all our romance book releases, eBook sales and promotions, sneak peeks and FREE romance books!

About the Author

Jambrea wanted to be the youngest romance author published, but life impeded the dreams. She put her writing aside and went to college briefly, then enlisted in the Air Force. After serving in the military, she returned home to Indiana to start her family. A few years later, she discovered yahoo groups and book reviews. There was no turning back. She was bit by the writing bug.

She enjoys spending time with her son when not writing and loves to receive reader feedback. She's addicted to the internet so feel free to email her anytime.

Jambrea loves to hear from readers. You can find her contact information, website details and author profile page at https://www.pride-publishing.com

www.ingramcontent.com/pod-product-compliance
Lightning Source LLC
Chambersburg PA
CBHW030139180626
46812CB00002B/760